DUPLICITY

BENSON FIRST RESPONDERS
BOOK 8

LISA PHILLIPS

eBook ISBN: 979-8-88552-197-0

Paperback ISBN: 979-8-88552-198-7

Published by Two Dogs Publishing, LLC. Idaho, USA

Cover Design by Sasha Almazan and Gene Mollica, GS Cover Design Studio, LLC

Edited by Janice Boekhoff, Lost Canyon Press Editing

Audiobook published by Recorded Books

DUPLICITY

ONE

"Don't do this." She grabbed Arlo's hand, but he pulled his arm away.

"You're not gonna stop me."

Fact was, he had no choice. He'd been ordered to do this, and since Arlo had a debt to pay, this was how he had to pay it.

His mother flopped down onto the ratty couch she always said was better than nothing. More times than not, it seemed like nothing was all they had. So, he'd gone out into the neighborhood and made his own way. She hadn't complained when he came home with rolls of bills. She took the money and didn't ask how he got it.

For a while, they had more food. Money for clothes, for her and Millie. He'd bought the sneakers he wanted. Took a girl out for a while, until she asked why he didn't treat her more fancy.

In the bedroom, Millie started crying. Dang kid was always wailing about something. Hard to believe she was his, but that was what Selise had said before she left the baby with his mother and never came back to pick her up.

He listened for a moment and looked around. Soaked up the sights and sounds he wouldn't know for a long time—maybe never.

If he was lucky, he'd get fifteen to twenty years. But when he got out, his debt would be paid, and he'd be free.

Millie didn't need to grow up with him in her life. He'd never done good for his daughter. His mom could make her own money for once. Even if Hayden had promised to "take care" of them, whatever that meant.

The two of them would be all right.

Arlo closed the front door behind him and headed down the hall. He took the stairs and went out the fire exit to the alley where a nice Dodge with black windows and an engine that growled was parked.

He got in the back, and it pulled out before he'd even shut the door.

"You know what you gotta do?"

Arlo stared up at the building. At the fire escape outside his window, where he and Selise had lain on that blanket and pretended they could see the stars.

"I asked you a question, kid."

He turned to the guy in the back seat beside him. Suit. Slick hair. Rings on both hands. Hayden was the kind of guy Arlo had tried to be, but some people had money. Some didn't. No matter how much Arlo tried, this kind of life took more than it gave. He weren't never gonna be rich.

"Yeah." He cleared his throat, but he sounded like a little kid anyway. "I know what I gotta do."

The guy up front drove the car from the east side of the

city, through downtown traffic, and right up to the curb in front of the Benson Police Department.

"So go do it."

Arlo turned to him. "Then we're clear?"

Hayden said, "Don't worry, kid. We'll take care of your momma and that baby."

"Whatever." He pushed out of the car and trudged up the steps. His last few moments of freedom for the rest of his life.

Not much of one. Wasn't ever gonna be something, hadn't ever been nothin' good anyways.

He stepped into the busy lobby of the department, walked by the glass windows—cops on one side, feds on the other—all the way up to the desk where a brother stood, stripes on his sleeves.

The guy looked nice enough. "Help you?"

Arlo lifted his chin, looked the guy in the eye, and said, "I'm the one who shot that cop."

TWO

Simon Olson had never understood his twin's drive to be an operator. Until a yard fight kicked off the first day of summer school before the bell ever rang.

He swung his leg over his motorcycle and removed his helmet, carrying it under his arm as he made his way across the parking lot to the courtyard in front of the school entrance. Backpack on. But he was here as a teacher, not a student.

The principal had asked him if he'd attended this school years ago, but he hadn't. There was no chance anyone here would recognize him. Simon had grown up a missionary kid in Malaysia. The fact he'd had a twin brother and an older sister were the only bright spots of his childhood.

The rest had been pretty much a nightmare.

He rolled his shoulders, and the buttoned shirt he'd "borrowed" from his brother's closet pulled tight over the scars between his shoulder blades.

Two teen girls turned to look at him. One said something to the other, and he pretended not to notice the look they exchanged.

Behind them, in a circle of high school kids, two boys worked out whatever frustration they had going on. Probably the fact they'd been consigned to summer school in the first place.

A woman trotted down the front steps. "All right, break it up!"

That's her.

She had on the blue uniform all Benson PD officers wore, although sometimes she wore plain clothes to work. Catalina Alvarez was the School Resource Officer assigned to East Benson High. Dark hair tied back in a bun. Slender but with muscles, so she looked tough enough the teen boys didn't give her a hard time. He'd guess in different clothes, she could be feminine in a way he'd probably choke on his tongue.

Bad idea.

He'd stopped short of reading her entire file because her history was none of his business. He might be a hacker, but he wasn't nosy. Never mind that he'd stared at her photo for longer than was necessary—considerably longer than any of the photos of other staff here, or the ones in the kids' files.

His last relationship had been humiliating, and he wasn't in a hurry to repeat that experience anytime soon. Getting two-timed with his own twin and strung along by his boss's assistant hadn't been a shining moment. It was worse than landing in jail.

Nothing could distract him enough for him to lose focus on why he was here. Right now, he had a new boss. Jasper Hollingsworth ran Vanguard Private Security and Investigations these days. Jasper had a new assistant, Oliver, who seemed like a decent guy. And Simon had a score to settle.

If he cleared it up himself, then no one would need to know.

A third boy entered the fray. He grabbed one of the two

who were fighting and flung him at the cop. The boy slammed into her, and Officer Alvarez went down with a cry. The interceptor kicked and kicked at the kid on the ground, who curled up with his arms over his head.

Simon moved between them, shouldering the kid out the way with the help of his bike helmet. Not putting his hands on the kid, but also not letting him hurt the other one anymore. "Enough!"

It was his father's voice that came out of his mouth. Everything in front of him washed in a burst of colors. A flash, maybe. Someone had taken a photo? Simon shook off the reaction and watched the kid back away from him.

Officer Alvarez said, "In the principal's office. Now!" She ushered the two toward the door. "Disburse!"

Simon turned and held out his hand to the kid on the ground. The teen grabbed his wrist, and Simon hauled him up.

Before he could ask anything, Officer Alvarez said, "Go. Principal's office, now." Catalina—*Officer* Alvarez—jerked her thumb over her shoulder. "Everyone else, go to breakfast." Her attention slid through him, and she watched the students head inside.

She hadn't noticed him. But then, her head whipped around, and she twisted to look right at him. "First day?"

"Is it that obvious?" The sheepish look heating his face wasn't a lie. He was out of his element, despite all his prep. Why hadn't he figured out he would be nervous?

She grinned. "Well, stow it. They can smell fear."

"Seriously?"

Catalina Alvarez tipped her head back and burst out laughing.

Simon had to grin but refused to stare at her. He wasn't going to be labeled a creeper on his first day teaching Algebra

2 to high school students who'd failed it over the past school year.

Better to think about math than the cop walking alongside him. Her brother was a cop, too. Simon had only briefly met Romeo Alvarez, so that wasn't likely to impact his ability to do this job.

Just inside the doors, she said, "All the students eat breakfast before the start of the day. That's the deal. Most are on meal assistance anyway, and a donation covered the rest, so all of them get breakfast and lunch."

His stomach rumbled. He'd had bad coffee in his hotel room but hadn't eaten this morning.

"In twenty minutes, the bell will ring, and you'll be in room 6B. Down the hall, around the corner, to the right. Second door." She turned to him and stuck out her hand. "Officer Alvarez. I'll be around."

He shook her hand. "Mr. Norris. I'll be in 6B."

She smiled and headed off, making little noise as she strode down the hall. Presumably going to watch over the lunchroom where the kids ate.

"I see you met our SRO." The principal stepped out of the school office, holding a badge.

"I did." Simon nodded. "Thanks for approving this."

Dawnetta Cruise had a stocky, full figure and had to be at least five-ten. No way these kids would mess with her. When Simon had first come in to speak to her about the open position, and why she needed to hire the IT guy from Vanguard to fill it, she'd answered the phone and promptly left the interview to go into the hall and yell at a kid like a drill sergeant. The girl had been suspended for three days for shoving her teacher.

She shook his hand so hard he had to bite back the wince. "Here's your badge, Mr. Norris."

He hadn't told anyone his real name. Though, he figured being Silas Norris—courtesy of a connection to the Accountant's Office and their ability to craft completely anonymous fake IDs—was close enough that he wouldn't slip up by getting anyone who asked to call him Sie. Close enough to Simon that it wouldn't feel odd.

His twin brother, Peter, would've wanted to do this assignment himself. Which was why Simon didn't tell him where he was going. Certainly not on a backpacking trip to Wyoming—alone. Though, that was where he'd sent his cell phone in a package just in case anyone checked.

"Thank you. In 6B, is that right?"

The principal nodded. "Good luck." She snickered a little and turned back to the office. Two women behind the front desk quit talking when she stepped in and walked by them. He heard the door to her office close.

Don't go look in the lunchroom. He would only be trying to get a peek at Officer Alvarez again.

Instead, he headed for the classroom and switched the lights on. It was pretty sparse, rows of single desks for the students. A desk for him in the corner. A smart whiteboard he'd be able to connect with from the tablet in his backpack. He ignored the teacher's PC and slid out his laptop, using the Wi-Fi to connect to the school network. He used that to piggyback through a back door he'd created that let him into the Vanguard system.

With access to their network, he could use tools he'd gathered or built himself to access every phone connected to the school Wi-Fi.

Kids started to trickle in. Once they were all seated, he looked around. "All right." The chatter quieted somewhat. "I'm Mr. Norris. I love math, so that probably makes me insane, but you can just call me the Gatekeeper of Passing Grades. Or the Wizard of Algebra. I haven't decided yet."

Someone snickered.

As he spoke, he sent an app to each of their phones. "Grab out your cell phones. I know you're not supposed to have it on in class, but the first thing we're gonna do is a game, and you need your device. Unlock it and accept the app I just sent you."

Simon slid out the pen for his tablet and wrote a simple multiplication equation on the screen. As he wrote, it showed up on the board behind him. "Solve this on your phone and submit your answer."

Before he finished, some of the answers started popping up on the screen as shown by a little icon. "Later, you can change your name and add a profile photo. Though, I get final say on both, and I don't wanna see anything nasty."

Simon read over the answers and saw most of them had it right. A couple were wrong. He started to solve it with the calculations showing up on the screen, but incorrectly so he'd get one of the more popular wrong answers.

Someone made a noise, recognizing his error.

Simon stopped and looked at the student who'd noticed. "Tell me what I'm doing wrong."

"The six is negative, so your answer should be negative."

He spotted the recognition on a few faces. "Does anyone want to go in and edit their answer?" A couple of students did. "There's a bonus question in the bottom right corner if you want to level up while you're waiting."

"What does leveling up get us?" The male student in the back corner had almost a full beard and a scar through his left eyebrow.

Simon said, "Try it and find out."

He was being obstinate, but this kid was the one he'd

come here looking for. Simon had a shot at getting to the root of the poison in his life, and Justice Spears was directly grafted into that root.

He looked at the screen of his laptop and spotted one phone in the room that was on the Wi-Fi but not being used to play the game. Considering everyone had a phone out, that meant someone had a second phone.

Bingo.

Simon clicked on that phone and ran the program to put a virus on the device, which no one would ever find and which could never be traced back to him.

The game they were playing on the app didn't go any farther than purely math problems. He'd explained it all to the principal, assuring her he was in no way violating their privacy. The system would forget any phone that closed the app.

Except the one he was looking for.

"Okay, now that everyone has the right answer, we're moving on. There's a lot of ground to cover in this class and only a few weeks to do it."

At the edge of his awareness, someone walked by the door. Officer Alvarez, maybe. He refused to look. He wasn't a trained operative, but he had some instincts for this line of work. As for teaching, well, he'd only done a certain amount of research. Fortunately, the principal promised to give him pointers on anything she noticed. No reason to jerk the kids around by not knowing what he was doing as an educator.

He wiped the screen of his tablet and wrote a new problem, followed by two more. Which question tripped up the students would give him an indication of who understood what and where he needed to start filling in gaps in their learning.

The screen of his laptop flashed, signaling the target

phone was receiving a text. He continued teaching the class while his program wormed its way into a network Simon had programmed long ago. One he'd created. A phone system not tied to any known commercial network, operating entirely off Wi-Fi signals and the nearest cell tower when nothing else was available, finding signal like an untraceable parasite. It enabled criminals to communicate with no way for law enforcement to track them or gain information from their devices.

In a long list of Simon's transgressions, this was the one that caused others the most harm. Unless he could gain access and take it down from the inside.

Then he would finally be free of the guilt of what he'd done.

Simon had walked away from everything and everyone and gone completely under the radar to get this done. He *couldn't* fail.

If he did, then he could never face the life he'd built—and the people he cared about—again.

He may as well never come home.

Cat's mother always said the Lord blessed Cat with not being "unfortunate looking." Whatever on earth that meant, it hadn't helped her in her role as Officer Catalina Alvarez. No matter what her brother Romeo thought of using his good looks to get suspects to confess and witnesses to cooperate.

Cat sat back in the chair in her office and stared at the monitor of her computer. Halfway through writing up a report on the fight that occurred this morning in the court-yard, she'd looked him up.

The new math teacher.

Mr. Silas Norris. Washington State University, teacher certificate. Some experience, but not much. He checked all the boxes. The background he'd submitted on his resume was clean. She wasn't going to wonder if it was "too clean." He was just a teacher.

He certainly was handsome. Something she'd been considering far too much rather than actually writing her report. Definitely not *unfortunate looking*. This Sunday at their family dinner, she was going to talk to her mother about that entire thing and how she didn't like it. People couldn't help what they looked like, and everyone was beautiful in a way. Variety was lovely. Everyone in the world was a little different from the person beside them, even identical twins.

Her hip and thigh started to ache, so she pushed her chair back and stood. Both palms on the desk, she stretched her right leg forward and back, grabbed her foot and held it behind her so she could stretch her hip flexor.

The spot where she'd been shot had gone from a localized stabbing pain to a general ache that only occasionally bothered her. She might never run a marathon, but she'd been able to pass the physical qualification for the police department six months after nearly losing her leg.

She turned to the small one-cup coffeemaker and put a pod in.

While it trickled and sputtered into the cup, a memory surged from deep in her psyche. A flashback was what her trauma counselor had called it. Better not to fight it. Instead, she let the past come back to her mind.

"Go right. I'll take the middle."

"Copy that." Catalina held her gun up, taking the measured steps she'd been taught in the academy. All of it becoming instinct until she barely had to think about her foot placement. She could hear the feminine whimper to her right, one aisle over.

She passed the nuts and chips and headed toward the counter, where a pool of blood already seeped out from behind the register.

The cashier was dead, or he would be in minutes if they didn't resolve this.

"Benson Police Department!" Sergeant Ellis, her training officer, would be approaching the suspect from the aisle to her left, leaving Cat to flank him and provide cover fire.

She picked up her pace and peered around the end of the aisle.

At the far side of the store, by the window, a woman sat with her knees up, her child gathered to her front. Both were crying silently, but Cat didn't see any blood.

The suspect backed up, moving erratically. Sweeping his arm around with the gun pointed nowhere and everywhere.

"Put the weapon down!" Sergeant Ellis's order rang through the store. "Put it down, now!"

The suspect had a hood up, so she couldn't make out his features. Just enough to know he was young. African American. Maybe late teens. A kid who'd seen too much and done some things no one knew. "Back up! Don't make me shoot you!"

"Don't throw your life away, kid!" Ellis yelled. "Put the gun down."

His movements grew even more erratic. His body language signaled the moment things took a turn. There was a decision made, and his limbs tightened. The gun came up.

Cat had to fire wide, or she could potentially hit an innocent or shatter the window and hit someone outside. She squeezed the trigger of her gun at the same time his went off.

Ellis screamed. A shot fired wild from the aisle beside her. The suspect spun around. A muzzle flashed. The noise eclipsed everything in her ears. Shoved with force, her legs crumpled under her.

Cat's back hit the floor, and her ears seemed to register sound again.

Someone else screamed.

Footsteps beat a path to the door. Cat moved, and excruciating pain burned in her leg. She touched it and found wet warmth. Blood.

"Ellis!" She gasped. "I'm hit! Ellis!"

She needed to...

She should...

Cat fumbled for her radio, her hand slick with blood. She squeezed the sides. "Unit twelve. Officer down!"

She had to get to her partner. She rolled, screaming as pain tore through her, and used her elbows to pull herself across the floor. More screaming, but from the woman and child. Cat forced the sound out of her mind and focused on her elbows. Move. Slide. Elbows.

Get to...

Her partner lay halfway down the aisle, blood around him. His neck.

"Sarge!" Catalina slid all the way to him and levered herself up enough to see he was practically gray. Lifeless eyes stared up at the ceiling.

She grasped the front of his vest and choked out a sob. "Sarge—"

"Alvarez."

She spun to find the principal in the doorway. "Ms. Cruise."

How long had she been standing there?

Cat lifted her coffee, careful not to slosh any on her hand or her uniform. "What can I help you with?"

Asking the question helped anchor her in the here and now. Instead of dwelling on the lingering issue of the shooter's identity. Or the teen who had confessed to the crime. The fact it had all seemed too easy to her. Too neat.

Even if everyone else thought it was resolved, she wasn't going to let it go.

She couldn't.

Principal Cruise grabbed the back of one of the two chairs Cat had facing her desk. "Just a quick note on our new math teacher."

"Mr. Norris?" She wasn't going to tell the principal what they'd talked about outside. That Cat might actually have *flirted* with the guy. Which was nuts and also a completely terrible idea. He might intrigue her, but given every relationship she'd ever had only ended in heartbreak and disaster, she wasn't ready to go through that again. No matter if it was good for a while before it went bad. Even if it could be *very* good.

It would always go bad.

Principal Cruise squeezed the back of the chair so hard the stuffing might burst out of the fake leather. "He's here only for the summer and promised not to leave us in the lurch. But the truth is, he's a *Vanguard agent.*" She whispered the last two words, glancing back over her shoulder when she was done.

Catalina frowned. "What does Vanguard want with the school?"

The private security and investigations company got into all kinds of crazy things, but over here on the east side of the city, she lived in a kind of cocoon where most of that stuff, thankfully, didn't touch her.

No bombings. No Russian criminals.

No snipers or building fires.

Absolutely no assassins.

Principal Cruise said, "He's here to gather intel for an ongoing investigation. He'll be recording license plate numbers of cars that pick students up and information on anyone hanging around too much, then sending that information back to his office. He'll run traces for a certain kind of phone the police can't access—" She waved at Cat, then continued, "Untraceable phones that aren't connected to the regular network."

That, at least, Cat had heard about. Though only a brief

mention. She should ask her brother about it. "One of the kids has an untraceable phone?"

"Evidently." The principal nodded.

"Why not just get a warrant and confiscate the phone?"

That's what a police investigation would entail. Not spying and reporting in. The police did solid work that held up in a court of law. Where people were given a fair chance to defend themselves.

Principal Cruise shrugged. "That's all the information I have, but I felt it important to keep you in the loop."

"Thank you. I appreciate that."

What she *wanted* to say was, "How much did Vanguard donate to the school?" Instead, she kept her mouth closed.

Who was Vanguard targeting here? Maybe they didn't know which kid had the phone.

Principal Cruise said, "Great. I appreciate your support."

She trailed out and left the door open. Catalina stared at the hall outside. Something was going on in her school? She needed all the information, not just what Vanguard wanted to trickle down—just enough to satisfy the questions, but not enough to invite curiosity.

That might have satisfied Principal Cruise, but not her.

Cat sent in her report and grabbed her coffee, locking her computer so no one could access it without knowing her password. Which only made her think...what if the Vanguard agent did? He surely had the tech to hack whatever he wanted. Maybe they'd already read her files.

He would know all about her investigation into Sergeant Ellis's death. How she'd never let go of the question of who the teen had been that pulled the trigger. And why she didn't truly believe it was the action of the kid who'd confessed, been tried as an adult, and sent to prison.

She might not be a good cop. Everyone in her life had told

her not to apply after Romeo was nearly killed in an explosion. Then, they told her to quit after she was shot. But she was a good School Resource Officer. She knew kids, and the one who was convicted of shooting her *wasn't* the person who'd killed her partner.

There was something not right about all of it.

Cat sipped her coffee as she walked a circuit of the school, outside to in. Sometimes, she did it in reverse. Then, there was the figure-eight loop on days when she was bored of choosing between left and right. Making sure her movements couldn't be predicted. There was always something to check on in a high school. Especially in summer, when troublemakers thought no one was here.

She prayed as she walked, asking for protection over the school. For wisdom to spot issues before they arose so she would be the kind of person who saw the signs and stepped in.

She prayed for the kid in prison, serving time for a crime she was certain he hadn't committed. For justice to be brought down on the real shooter, a man who had changed her life forever and destroyed a family. Ellis's kids had to grow up without a father, and his wife had to live with a hole in her heart.

She prayed for the Vanguard agent.

Up ahead, a teen swept out of the bathroom, grinning and flushed red. Definitely, a troublemaker.

"Saraya. How are you today?"

The girl only snorted and sauntered past Catalina, back to class.

Cat sipped her coffee and hung around in the hall outside the bathroom. A minute or so later, another girl left, swiping her sleeve under her eyes. She spotted Cat and realized she was busted. "How are you, Taylor? Everything okay?"

"Oh, I'm fine, Cat. Thanks." Some of the kids called her Officer Alvarez, but the ones she got to know called her Cat.

They'd talked a few times before, after the teacher reported indications that Taylor had been cutting herself. The meeting with Taylor and her mother had been a cry fest, and the girl had improved after that. Taylor was seeing a counselor outside of school. There was reason to be optimistic.

"My door is always open, you know that."

"K, thanks." Taylor ducked her head and went back to class.

Cat said another prayer. For the teens who came and went from this building. Prayer was a full-time job. She'd have to figure out when to get to the bottom of this Vanguard thing. And the investigation she kept hidden on her computer.

She definitely didn't have time to be distracted by a good-looking guy.

It would only spell trouble.

FOUR

Simon stepped outside to watch the students leave in cars, on the bus, or get picked up by parents. One kid rode past on a bicycle, his helmet unbuckled. The kind of upbringing Simon had never experienced.

"You're looking at them like you've never seen anything like this."

He pretended not to be startled and shifted the laptop closer to his front. He needed proximity to keep the connection going until his program could worm its way into Justice Spears's GPS. Officer Alvarez stood beside him.

He tried to act nonchalant about it. "I never went to school. I was a missionary kid." He swallowed down the lump in his throat. "My mom homeschooled us."

"So you have siblings?" she asked. "I have a brother. He's a cop. My dad was a cop, before he retired. My uncles were all cops."

"The family business?"

"Except if you're female." She winced. "They're not sexist, just overprotective. How about you?"

Simon smiled as much as he could. "My mom passed

away, and my dad—" He couldn't even finish that sentence. "I have an older sister and a twin brother."

"Wow." She smiled back. "People used to ask if Romeo and I were twins since we were in the same grade. He's older, almost a year. Do you and your brother look alike?"

"Some people can't tell us apart." Simon ran a hand through his hair. "He cut his short for work, so I let my hair grow. It's easier for now."

And yet, part of him resented accommodating others in this way. The resemblance was his connection with Peter. It was something they shared that was theirs alone and no one else's.

Peter having a fiancée didn't change that. But it seemed like it changed everything else. Nothing had really been the same since Lena two-timed them. Peter had changed departments and then met Selena. Simon's life hadn't altered all that much. So why did things seem…off?

"That's cool." She seemed like she was genuinely interested. "And you work for Vanguard?"

Simon nearly choked. "Principal Cruise told you."

"I am the School Resource Officer. I need to know these things."

"So now you know." He checked the screen of his laptop and saw Justice had left and was headed north toward a residential area—or the freeway onramp.

The rumble of an engine reached the edge of his awareness.

Simon spun to see a black SUV with tinted windows roll past, slowing as it hit the school zone. But there seemed to be something far more ominous about it than simply the driver wanting to obey the flashing signs to slow down.

"Everything okay?"

He barely registered her question. Simon tracked the

SUV past the school until it turned the corner at the end of the street.

"Silas?"

Okay, he didn't like being called the wrong name. "Sie is fine."

"Cat." An interested, curious look crept into her expression.

As much as Simon wanted to talk to her more, he had to do his job, or he would never end this. "I should go."

"Hot date?" As soon as the words left her mouth, she flushed.

Did she think he was some kind of ladies' man? Everyone he knew thought he was a super nerd. Math teachers weren't known for being athletic, but that was a stereotype. Kind of like what people thought of homeschoolers.

He stared at her. "No, I don't have a date."

Then Simon turned away and went back to the class. He grabbed his things and shut the lights off, leaving out a side door that meant he had to walk around the corner of the building to get to his bike. He adjusted the backpack straps and slid on his helmet.

The roar of the engine under him. The helmet muted the world aside from that. All of it was a sensory rest he needed after spending a long morning with people, having their attention on him, and knowing if he didn't succeed at this job, then he might as well forget everything.

Walk away from all of it.

He weaved through traffic, picking up speed on long straight stretches. Until he checked himself because he was in danger of being pulled over. It could be a cop he knew—which would be awkward when he gave them Silas Norris's driver's license.

Simon worked hard to get Catalina Alvarez out of his

head. If he spent more time with her, he was going to be in trouble. Cat was absolutely the kind of woman who could test his resolve. Crazy beautiful, astute enough to call him on his mini freakout about that SUV. She was a cop, which meant she valued doing what was right. He didn't know her history or why she was an SRO, but it didn't make a difference. No matter which way it shook out...

Bad idea.

If anyone was going to change his mind, it was her. And that was exactly why he was going to keep it professional, with a side of actively avoiding her. After all, when she found out the truth of who he was and even a slice of what he'd done since he had figured out he was good with computers, she would run away as fast as she possibly could, and he would be left with a broken heart.

Again.

GPS in his helmet speakers directed him to the spot where Justice had driven in his old Mustang. It turned out to be a body shop with a car garage next to it advertising twenty-minute oil changes.

No one touched Simon's bike but him, so he pulled into the diner across the street. He might need a signal boost, but it was close enough to the kid's location and the phone his laptop was still connected with.

Or it would be as soon as he got on the diner's Wi-Fi.

Simon slid into a booth and ordered a big enough all-day breakfast special that he wasn't going to need dinner later.

"Coffee?"

"Yeah, thanks."

The grizzly-looking waitress said, "Sure thing," in a voice that betrayed how long she'd smoked.

Simon opened his laptop, angling it so no one would see what he was working on. The waitress poured him some coffee, and Simon said thank you while he stuck his earbuds in. Rather than leaving them in with no music playing—which he did a lot so he could focus—he connected his laptop to the phone across the street and switched on the microphone.

He used a noise filtering app to isolate the voices and clean up the feed enough that he could turn up the volume and hear snatches of conversation.

Justice was humming. A compressor hummed in the background.

A message popped up on his computer. Peter had sent a text to his phone, the one he'd mailed to Wyoming. The communication had grown sparse over the last week, which sort of meant his brother knew something was up—but he'd also give Simon space until he was ready to talk about it. Maybe Pete was suspicious of his sudden need to "disconnect" and vacation by himself, or perhaps he had figured out Simon was nowhere near Yellowstone.

Simon pulled a photo from the folder where he'd stashed images of the national park taken from social media. He hadn't bothered to use a design program to superimpose his picture onto the image of the scenery. Peter would see right through it.

He sent the image in reply and told Peter he was good. Because that, at least, was true.

Through his headphones, he heard laughter, the kind that followed an inappropriate joke or one told at someone's expense.

"Guess you'd better pass school so you can be a big shot like the old man." Male voice. Not Justice.

"I will. Don't sweat it." The response came from the teen who'd been in his class this morning.

"You think he'll let you go if you don't do what he wants?"

Simon stilled. Everything in him reacted, making him want to run as far and as fast as he could.

Justice asked, "So, I don't get what I want?" The question was issued like a challenge. He wanted the man talking to him to believe he was big-time.

The person Justice was talking to laughed. "Oh, you'll get what you want. Don't worry. We'll take care of you."

"It better be a good birthday."

"Didn't I just say I'd take care of you?"

Justice asked, "You wanna be my lieutenant when I take over, Hayden? Is that it?"

"You think I've been watching your butt for years for my own amusement?"

"Like you didn't get something out of it?" Justice chuckled.

"That's why I'll make it good for you on your birthday. That way it's good for me. We both get what we want. And when the time comes, yeah, I wouldn't mind being your lieutenant. If it works out that way."

Justice said, "Then report in. Tell him I went to school like a good little boy."

A power tool buzzed across the audio feed, breaking through the filter. Simon winced and turned down the volume.

The person Justice was with would be contacting the old man. Did that mean he also had a phone connected to Simon's system?

He checked for a reply to the photo he'd sent Peter, but his brother had seen the message and didn't send anything back. At least, not yet.

It was a risk doing this whole thing. Trying to fly under the radar. Peter had as much skill as Simon did with computers even if he'd chosen to be an operator instead.

The bubble would burst eventually. His brother would figure out where he was, and Vanguard would know he'd gone off on his own to solve this. But it didn't have anything to do with them. This was about righting what he'd done wrong so he could be the person he wanted to be without the stain.

If he wanted redemption, Simon had to get it for himself.

His father had attempted to beat sinlessness into them, all the while corrupting others and making money from it. He'd had Simon's mother murdered when she found out what he was really doing. And it certainly hadn't been God's work.

Simon had left all that behind, and now he decided for himself. No one got to tell him what to do, not even God. Peter might have resolved the question enough to give his life to the Lord, but as far as Simon could see, that just meant being told what to do, how to live.

He had freedom now.

For the first time in his life, he had control over what he did and the choices he made, and he wasn't going to give that up to anyone.

The burner phone he'd bought under this new alias rang in his pocket. He only had it because not having a cell phone in this day and age would be more obvious.

He looked at the screen. Local area code—for the west side of Washington state. He knew that number...

Simon pulled out one earbud and answered it. "Hello?"

"Boy, you're not foolin' anyone. What do you think you're doing?" Her voice rang in his head, attachment and friend-ship, care and mutual respect. Talia was the one person who could call him on his crap and get him to at least think about changing his mind.

"T—"

"No." She cut him off. "Don't make me hike all the way to

Benson in these heels. I'll miss putting my kids to bed tonight, and it'll be *your fault*."

Simon closed his eyes. "I know what I'm doing."

"I sure hope so. Traipsing around in that system, poking. Someone's gonna notice."

"I'll be done by then."

Talia sighed. "I hope you'll not be done because you got dead." She muttered something and hung up.

Simon stared at the phone. It was just Talia who had noticed. Considering who she was and the fact she gave him a run for his money in the computer hacking department, it didn't mean he was risking too much. She cared. That was all.

Which was why he had to do this.

So he'd get the chance to prove he could be someone worth caring about.

If he didn't *get dead* before that happened.

FIVE

F ive minutes before the end of the day bell, Catalina's desk phone rang. "Officer Alvarez."

"It's me."

Cat frowned. "What do you want, Romeo?" She rolled her eyes, not in the mood for her brother right now.

"Something afoot at the high school?"

Surprisingly, he didn't make a comment about the rough area the school was located in. "Just learning, as per usual."

Romeo snorted.

"Day off?"

"I'm on nights this rotation. Four months of not seeing the sun except while I'm trying to sleep."

"Come to the dark side. We have cookies and daylight."

He snorted.

"Anything new on the streets?" Things had been pretty crazy in Benson with the Russians. A limo bombing the past summer. A medical center that turned out to be connected to organized crime. A drive-by mass shooting aimed at cops where both she and Romeo had ended up helping out in the aftermath. Thankfully unscathed by the flying bullets, they'd triaged a friend who had been bleeding badly.

She'd mostly managed to hide her reaction to the blood and the sounds.

The next day, she'd gone in and seen the department therapist. She kept that up weekly for a couple of months and had her last one the previous week. Since the shooting, she'd kept attending the group she went to for trauma survivors, even if sometimes she only got to it once a month.

Romeo said, "Got some chatter about a new dealer coming in from Canada."

She gripped the phone and leaned back in her chair. "A new substance?"

There had been so much shifting of power in the criminal world in Benson over the last year or two that it was hard to keep up with who was the latest bigshot.

The last kingpin had terrorized a lot of people before he was finally taken down.

"Not that we know of. Same old poison." Romeo sounded like he was walking, maybe taking his dog out. Her brother got home at seven in the morning when he worked nights and usually slept until one. She needed more sleep than that, but he'd always been wired to need less.

Should she ask him the question burning in her mind? This was just her brother. There weren't many people in the world she could share her true feelings with, but with Romeo, she could.

At least, some things.

He'd agreed with her that the conviction of her "shooter" seemed too easy, but he also wasn't as determined as her to find the real killer. He seemed satisfied to let it lie. Like everyone else.

"Rome, what do you know about Vanguard?"

"Why do you ask?"

Cat said, "That doesn't matter. Just tell me what you know about them."

His voice grew breathy. He must have switched to running, which meant he had his headphones in and his phone in his pocket. His dog was an old lab, but she still loved to run.

Pretty much every female in existence loved Romeo Alvarez. It had been annoying in high school when all her friends just wanted to know if he was single. Romeo hadn't cared much about whether he was or not, he went out with whoever whenever. Thankfully, adulthood seemed to have mellowed him—some.

"Vanguard does great work. They have teams all over, not just in Benson. But the crew that works locally are solid. All the ones I've met."

"You know a guy named Silas Norris?"

"Nope. Never heard of him."

The bell rang down the hall, followed by a rush of feet. Conversation. Lockers slamming. The kids could never get out of school fast enough, although there were always a few who seemed content to linger. Their home lives were probably messed up. Not everyone was blessed with parents who cared about them or their education.

"I should go. The bell just rang."

Romeo asked, "Meet me for lunch?"

Cat started to answer but caught herself before saying she had a "date." An appointment was a better description. Or a meeting? He'd think she was seeing the department shrink if she said that. "I have a thing this afternoon."

"Does it have anything to do with the fact Thursdays are visiting days at the prison?"

The place where the kid who shot her and killed her partner had been sent.

"Cat?"

She said, "I just want to see if he's all right."

"You don't need to do that. There are family members of inmates who work every day to make conditions better so it's humane."

True, but it didn't hurt to check. Make sure he wasn't being treated like an animal. Whether it was for a mistake or a willfully committed crime didn't matter. People had the right to basic respect, regardless. A sentiment some cops didn't necessarily share.

"It's not about the prison," she said. "It's about the fact he didn't shoot me."

"You're one hundred percent certain of that?" He said it fast because he'd said it to her so many times. Enough that he already knew the answer.

"I'm hanging up now."

"I'll see you later."

"Yeah, maybe."

His "see you later" meant a combination of "I love you" and "bring me dinner if you're out later because I'm a helpless male who can't feed myself."

Cat hung up, knowing her "yeah, maybe" meant exactly that.

Their shorthand wasn't always understood by others. But when Romeo had flat out told her he didn't like her last boyfriend, there had been no confusion.

Pastor Tyler Cunningham of the local church here on Eastside that had broken away from the larger Benson Community Church hadn't ever been good enough for Cat in her brother's eyes. Now that it was over, she could spend the rest of her life analyzing and overanalyzing what happened between her and the guy who ran their youth ministry.

From the night they'd met at a big Christian music concert through the rush of multiple dates a week for months. The red flags hadn't seemed like flags at the time.

Cat wrapped up her workday and signed out, then she drove her little Toyota over to the prison. It was for the best that she didn't see Silas—Sie—outside the school. The last thing she needed was another relationship that would seem great on the surface but underneath held nothing resembling a solid foundation.

The drive was at least an hour, but to keep from getting sucked into thinking about the whole of what had happened, she flipped on a radio station that played sermons and turned up the guy with the Scottish accent.

When would she get what she wanted? To travel. To get married and have kids.

To have the work she did make a difference.

Most of all, to get justice for her partner.

All of it was in God's control, but as happened so often, it seemed as if He held His hand closed when it came to her. Cat's mom always reminded her to be diligent and faithful, but when it had been so long, it was hard to keep the faith.

She felt dry.

Like she was missing something that seemed to come so easily to others.

Cat took the exit off the freeway, whispering her prayers to the solitude of her car. She checked in at the prison and left nearly everything with the desk. No weapons. No phone. She'd worn plain clothes today, so anyone seeing her talking to the kid wouldn't necessarily think she was a cop.

He dragged his limbs into the room, shackled hands and feet. The peace officer accompanying him connected the shackles to the other side of the booth. Thick clear plastic between them.

That's hardly necessary. The kid wasn't violent.

She had looked his history up, so that might not be the truth. He may very well be violet when provoked. Now that he'd spent months in prison, his instincts were likely wound even tighter. He might not be a threat to her, given the protections separating them, but he was a threat, nonetheless. A convicted cop killer.

His hair had grown out since court. He looked younger in a lot of ways, and in others, much older. Catalina wasn't going to ask how he was being treated because she doubted she'd get a straight answer out of his mouth.

She lifted the phone and held it to her ear. When he did the same, she said, "Hey, Arlo."

His dark eyes stared at her, unblinking. A muscle in his jaw flexed. "What do you want?"

Not many inmates were visited by the person they'd shot. She couldn't blame him for always asking the question. He seemed more like one of the kids at the school rather than a hardened criminal.

"Did you think about what books you might want me to bring you?"

Arlo shrugged one shoulder.

"I read a great book a couple of weeks back. Military guys in this unit that retrieves artifacts from around the world that have properties that make them...magical. Some of them. Others were crazy inventions that were supposed to have been taken apart in, like, the Dark Ages. They get them out of the hands of evil people bent on destroying the world. I could bring some of those. I have the whole series."

He shrugged again.

"Have you seen your mom lately, or Millie?"

"The baby ain't comin' here. I don't wanna see her." His tone tightened as he spoke, and he never relaxed.

Grief, not just for her partner, welled up in her. So many lives had been affected by what happened. "Do you need anything?"

He lifted his brows and shot her a look. "From you?"

"Because we could trade. Since there's plenty I want from you."

He frowned. "Like what?"

"How about the truth, for starters. Or the name of the person who ordered you to confess to a crime you didn't commit."

He started to shift in his seat.

She ignored it. "Perhaps why you'd feel like this was your only choice. I want to ask if you know who actually shot my partner and shot me because that person should be the one sitting across from me."

His expression shuttered. Not that it had every truly opened. He wasn't in a situation where he could let his guard down enough to display his true feelings. "What's done is done."

"I'm not letting this go."

"Say what you want. Show up how many times you want. I'm not gonna tell you nothin' besides what I told my lawyer. I shot two cops because I *could*. Because cops deserve to die." He slammed the phone down and called out to the guard, who led him out.

Cat replaced the phone and sat back in the chair.

He'd made his choice. Things were done, and he didn't see how they could be changed. By all rights, she should let him live this life he seemed determined to stay stuck in. As if he had no choice, or as if the outcome had already been decided for him.

No one else saw a point to pursuing this, but something in her refused to let it go.

She signed out and got her things, stepping out into the late afternoon sun. The rush of summer warmth after the air-conditioning inside hit her like a wave. She needed a vacation but only had a week off between the end of summer school and the start of the new year prep for teachers before the kids came back.

She slid into the driver's seat and turned on the engine to push out the sweltering air in here. The radio came on full volume, and the pastor being broadcast now read a verse about sin and its destructive ability. The way it tore apart lives and families—unless confession was made.

She leaned her head back against the seat and felt tears roll down her face. *I haven't done anything wrong.*

So why did she feel this way?

SIX

Simon rode his motorcycle into the parking lot of the hotel where he was currently staying at a little after six. Dinner was the fast-food sub sandwich in his backpack, which he'd bought after a long ride to clear his head.

He hadn't seen the School Resource Officer except across the schoolyard today. Not Cat. Not even Officer Alvarez. She was only the SRO. Otherwise, this thing where he was thinking about her way too much would get even worse. She could genuinely mess up his plan at the school.

It was far better all around to steer clear of her.

Keep his head down.

Get the job done.

Sweat lined the inside of his riding jacket, but he wouldn't go without it. He unzipped it now. Sandwich. Shower.

He sent Talia a text that he would be thirty minutes tops. They would both log in, and he'd have someone else to ensure he didn't miss anything while he worked through the system.

An unease crept up his back, some instinct flared to life, but he didn't look up from the phone at first. He stowed it in his back pocket and only then took a second to glance around under the guise of gathering his things from the bike and securing it.

Maybe he should've paid attention when his twin tried to teach him those operator skills. Situational awareness. They had buzzwords for everything. When the team from Last Chance County—Chevalier Protection something—had visited, it had been like listening to another language.

A few months ago, he'd been hit over the head and tied up. Kidnapped. Forced to ride around in the back of an SUV while a criminal kingpin explained that Simon worked for him now. That he would be moved from place to place, forced to work on whatever tech thing they needed, and probably sold to someone else. Traded around until he killed himself or was killed.

The ordeal had ended in a vehicle crash where the SUV flipped, and Peter dragged him to safety.

Things didn't end that well every time. Like seven years ago, when he'd first been forced to create the program for the phone system. Even if Peter saved him just a few months ago, he wouldn't always be able to do it.

Sometimes, Simon had to save himself.

His goals might not matter if someone moved in with ideas of their own about what he should be doing. And right now, he was tired of it all. Tired of fearing things he couldn't control, always looking over his shoulder, wondering when the next bad guy would show up with a gun. He had to take the system down, kill the whole communication network, and show anyone who cared to look into him what he could do.

He jogged up the stairs to four, then down the hall to his room. The key card was on an app on his phone, so Simon held it up to the reader and pushed into the room. Nicer than anyplace he'd ever lived if he was willing to admit—

Someone was inside the room.

Simon dropped his backpack, probably squashing the sandwich. His helmet bounced on the floor in a way that didn't sound good. He crouched and came back up with his knife out at the same second the door clicked closed.

"Whoa. Easy." Jasper Hollingsworth sat in the armchair in the corner. "I'm glad that isn't a gun."

"Because I might have already shot you?" Maybe he should get one, but that meant learning how to use it, and guns freaked him out. Stabbing someone was a bit grizzly, which just made it a good threat. "What do you want, Jasper?"

He wore a suit, the way he had during his time as a police detective. But now Jasper was transitioning into the role of Vanguard CEO. Otherwise known as Simon's new boss.

"Silas Norris? Clever. Actually, the entire ID is airtight. I never would have found you."

So how had he?

"That's the idea." Simon set his backpack on the bed, the damp shirt clinging to his upper body. He would unlace his boots and take them off, but the smell would permeate the room. He'd rather do that with the window cracked. "It's supposed to make it so no one finds me. That way I get actual peace and quiet."

"It's not a Vanguard ID. And yet, you're on a Vanguard job?" Jasper kept his feelings about it under wraps, giving nothing away in his expression. "Except I have nothing open on my desk with your name on it, and Peter thinks you're backpacking in Wyoming. He showed me a picture just this morning."

They both knew Peter wasn't a hundred percent fooled. He just wasn't pressing it. He would let Simon do what he needed to and probably figured Simon would call when he needed to.

Simon's smartwatch vibrated on his wrist. He turned it to see what the alert was for—his computer had connected to the internet here at the hotel and the worm's progress into the communication network had been completed.

"I have work to do." His way of asking Jasper to get out.

"Not for me you don't," Jasper said. "You're moonlighting?"

Simon shook his head.

"So Romeo was right. There's a Vanguard operation going on at the school where his sister is the SRO."

If the guy ever came by the school, Cat's brother would recognize Simon right away. She would find out who he really was and that he'd lied. Maybe he didn't need to worry about that now. Considering his cover had already been blown.

"It's personal."

"And you're telling people it's a Vanguard case? That gives us a problem, Sie." Jasper shifted to sit forward, elbows on his knees. "It makes Vanguard liable if anything happens, and you're missing resources we could provide. Help we *want* to give."

"I don't need anything." He needed to do this on his own, without interference. It would be better if the least number of people possible knew what he was doing. Which was why he'd done it this way, keeping things quiet. His business didn't need to be public knowledge.

Jasper shook his head. "Why are you lying to everyone?"

"I'm not..." He had no way to defend himself. Probably because he *was* lying. Jasper wasn't his father—Simon wasn't going to get beaten for twisting the truth or pretending that what he'd said wasn't a lie. There was no physical threat here.

And yet, another bead of sweat ran down his back and he had to keep his hands clenched to keep them from shaking.

"Clare never micromanaged me."

"This isn't micromanaging you. You work for me now, and this is how I do things. Without anyone falling through the cracks."

"Clare didn't tell me what I could and couldn't do."

Jasper said, "I'm aware Clare rarely had to assign you tasks. She holds you in high regard, and you've more than proven yourself."

"So why can't you accept that I know what I'm doing?"

"Oh, I know you know what you're doing." Jasper stood. "It's how you're going about it, Sie. Lying. Putting yourself at risk so if anything happens no one even knows there's something wrong. The company works when we pull together to get things done."

He'd come from the police department and SWAT to work at Vanguard, so Jasper was all about a team mentality. It wasn't surprising this had come out of his mouth, but Simon didn't have time for the "stronger together" speech. He was hot, sweaty, and hungry, and he had work to do.

Simon said, "This is something I have to do by myself."

Jasper looked almost sad, which didn't make sense. "You've been different since Marcus Harper abducted you. Everyone knows it, and Peter is worried about you. He thought it was a good thing you're taking a break."

"I am taking a break—from having everyone breathing down my neck at work."

Didn't they know enough about him to accept what he needed to do? Simon had never pushed his own agenda before, but this time was different than any other. Clare had given him a choice to go to juvenile detention all those years ago. That day felt like another lifetime now. She'd offered him and Peter an internship on the understanding they'd finish school and get good grades, turn their lives around.

She'd offered him a choice he hadn't expected.

He'd paid her back tenfold by being the best employee he could be. Keeping his nose clean. Being an invaluable part of the team at Vanguard so his life never made another turn that took away his choices. He hadn't had any choices growing up. He refused to give them up now.

"I want an email in my inbox by nine tomorrow morning explaining the ins and outs of every single part of this. If you don't want me to tell your brother you're lying to him, that's fine. But my people don't operate without backup, and if there was a case so personal you couldn't let it go, then you should've told someone so they could help you."

"I don't need help. I'm doing fine."

Jasper shifted his stance. "Yeah? That's why you came in here and pulled a knife? Because things are fine? I could've shot *you*."

Guns never solved anything. He'd had more than enough pointed at him, been threatened more times than he could count, and sat alone in the dark wondering when he would lose his life.

All of it reminded him far too much of the way his father had "raised them" in the way the Lord intended—according to Dear Old Dad—and how he strived not to spare the rod. Discipline had been their salvation.

Simon rolled his shoulders.

A grown man, not a scared child.

"I have it handled."

Jasper said, "You break my heart, kid."

He never would've said that to Peter. Everyone thought the sun shone on his brother, and he could do no wrong in their eyes. The bigshot operator with his bigshot missions.

Simon loved him, but next to Peter, he would always fail to measure up. How many times had his father told him he was the weaker vessel?

This case was his business. He was about to say that to Jasper when the guy shifted and pulled a folded paper out of the inside pocket of his suit jacket.

Simon stared at the offered paper.

"You will take it. You're going to attend four times, and then we're gonna talk about how your role at Vanguard will work going forward."

Simon snatched it out of his hand and unfolded the paper. "A trauma survivors group? Are you kidding me?"

"Four weekly meetings. You work this case, and when it's done, I'll make sure you still have a job." Jasper swept past him to the door. He didn't grasp the handle. He just turned back. "Something happened to you when Harper kidnapped you. Something you won't even talk to Peter about."

"I don't need anyone to worry about me."

"A lot of people care about you."

They shouldn't. Simon didn't say the words on the tip of his tongue. "I know what I'm doing."

"I sure hope so." Jasper grabbed the door. "First meeting is tonight."

"And if I don't go?"

"Then consider yourself fired."

The door clicked shut, and Simon was alone.

SEVEN

Days like today were why Catalina had started attending a group for survivors of trauma in the first place. These days, she went on occasion, but not with any regularity. With Romeo at work tonight, she'd decided to come—after all, her parents wouldn't want to see her like this.

Okay, maybe they did *want* to. But they didn't deserve her mood right now. They would try to comfort her, then she would break down more. Her father would retreat into his office. Her mom would treat her like a five-year-old with a skinned knee. Having to carry the weight of their concern wasn't something she could bear on top of her grief.

Cat stepped from the echoey hall into the small room in the community center where they held meetings like this. The group that conversed in sign language met next door because she'd gone in there by mistake once, and now she could sign the word *Sorry*.

There were a handful of people in the room. Regular attendance was about eight, plus Rebecca, who was the group leader and a family therapist with a specialty in trauma. The department shrink had passed on the information for the group not long after Cat finished physical therapy.

A man in his midtwenties stood talking to Rebecca, but it wasn't until she handed him a paper and he turned that Cat saw it was him. *Sie.* Silas Norris spotted her and flinched.

He recovered faster than her and sat in an open seat at the far end of the circle.

Rebecca moved to stand behind her chair. "Ladies and gentlemen, this is Simon Olson. He's visiting us tonight, and hopefully, more…"

Cat didn't hear what else Rebecca said. She whirled around and glared at *Simon.* Heat infused the skin of her cheeks. He'd given her a fake name? That was why his ID had seemed clean. Too clean.

She couldn't believe this.

Cat headed for the closest free chair. Someone stepped in front of her and took it. Then another seat filled. And another. The only remaining empty chair was the one beside him. Cat kept her head down and settled into it, smiling at the nurse to her left.

On her right, *Simon* had his phone in one hand and was tapping it against his leg. Was he going to do that the whole time? The fake name clearly meant that whatever happened at the school was only part of the mission. Was this going to be the real man behind the fake identity?

Rebecca had them go around and introduce themselves. Walter, an older man who had served in Vietnam and then got hooked on drugs and been homeless for a while, talked about his granddaughter's twelfth birthday party.

At the end, everyone was smiling.

Cat said, "That's a big change from the last time I was here. I'm glad I came back to listen."

Walter smiled. "It was a good day."

Rebecca had a couple more people share, and then she talked a little about positive habits and how to get rid of bad habits—by making them inconvenient. A few of the group members took notes.

Simon's phone buzzed. He glanced at the screen, and she saw the name *Talia*. Probably a woman in his life. Surely, Rebecca had told him there was a rule about not being on a phone during group time.

He typed a reply message.

> It's going down tonight then.

Cat frowned. She glanced at the young woman across the circle and listened for a bit about her baby son and how he was teething. She shared a smile with the woman.

Simon bounced his knee up and down. The real guy behind the fake persona seemed distracted. He didn't want to be here—which admittedly wasn't so dissimilar to her first time—but this seemed like a protest rather than a general reluctance.

What was his deal?

Rebecca sent Cat a knowing smile.

"Oh, no." Cat chuckled. Where Rebecca would normally invite a person to share whatever they wanted, her friend knew she could call on Cat to share something specific.

Simon shifted in his seat.

Rebecca pushed back a hank of her purple-tinted brown hair. "Catalina, I seem to recall you visiting us somewhat reluctantly the first time."

Cat laughed. "That's putting it mildly."

She'd squirmed. A lot like Simon had been doing. Along with being on his phone. This was a trauma survivors group, so if he stuck it out, he would find solutions for his need to disassociate by connecting instead with whoever was on his phone. She did it as well with social media and games that passed the time. A way to feel better. But it didn't solve the underlying problem.

Disassociation never did.

She said, "I'm happy to share something."

Simon glanced from his phone to her, but she didn't look back at him.

Rebecca lowered her clipboard to her lap. "Would you like to tell us how the group has helped you or something you might be struggling with at the moment?"

She could talk about Arlo and their conversation at the prison, but it was all a little too raw right now. She'd cried it out at the prison, sitting in her car waiting for the air-conditioning to cool the interior of her car.

The last thing she needed was to drag back up the details of a police investigation. Or speak in a way that let people believe the police had somehow covered up the truth.

That wasn't the case.

She only believed that enough people had taken the easy way out, the truth that amounted to the lowest common denominator. Figuring that the dangerous person was off the streets. Some kind of street justice. Did the details matter when everything was settled?

That line of thinking wasn't the way her father had raised her. Cat might not be a beat cop anymore, but that didn't mean she wouldn't keep working it.

"Cat?"

"Right." She cleared her throat.

Cat could put herself out there so Simon would be comfortable enough to talk about whatever it was he'd come here to share. A tiny note inside her said it might not be a coincidence that he showed up at her group tonight, of all nights, but the respect she had for this group meant she'd do what she could to help it work for him.

"This group probably saved my life," Cat said. "I was healed. Physically, anyway. PT was done, but the scar on my leg would never go away. Everyone seemed to expect me to be better, but I was still the rookie cop lying on the floor of that convenience store calling in an 'officer down.'"

Simon shifted in his seat.

"I'm always going to carry this scar." Cat touched the front of her hip, where it met her thigh. High on her leg was the visible reminder of her pain. So easy to cover it up with clothes. "But it's the brokenness on the inside that I'm still figuring out how to heal. Maybe it won't ever be completely gone."

She glanced at Simon then and would've sworn she saw a sheen of tears in his eyes. He glanced down at his lap.

Rebecca gave her a soft smile. "Some elements of what happened to us, we need to release. Some, we hold on to because it's what keeps us going and tethering ourselves to the good that we found in the middle of it—or the hope that exists in dark places."

"What if there's none of that?" Simon paused, as if he hadn't intended to say that. "What if there's no good? No hope?"

Cat turned to him and saw what existed in everyone who needed to be in this group. In him, it surprised her. The depth. The sorrow. Who was this man? He couldn't be more than twenty-four or twenty-five, about the same age as her. Why did it seem as though he was far older, maybe in experience? Trauma had aged him. Taken him places he never wanted to be.

For a second, it scared her.

Rebecca was talking, but Cat couldn't make out the words

that seemed to ring in her head. She was focused on him. She wouldn't invade his privacy, so if she was going to learn what had broken Simon Olson, then he would be the one to tell her.

And if he wanted to know her, then she would tell him everything she'd been through.

It could be a bad idea: two broken hearts trying to find healing. She was supposed to find that in Jesus, not in the good-looking man who sat beside her. Someone who could drag her down with his pain.

"I don't see how a group is going to help me 'find myself' or whatever this is." Simon shifted in his seat. "I'm just here so I don't lose my job."

His tone indicated he believed it was little more than a waste of time. But it wasn't Cat's job to convince him the group could be a huge help in freeing him from the past.

"I'm sure you'll find benefits even if you're only here to check a box," Cat said with all sincerity, mostly because she was convinced that he would have a breakthrough soon.

But this cemented it for her. He wasn't the guy she needed in her life to lean on and find contentment with. Simon might be good-looking, and if he worked for Vanguard, then he'd been vetted, but she just couldn't jeopardize her own recovery with someone so new in theirs. If he even wanted to heal.

They could be friends, but she couldn't risk any more with her history.

Simon only shrugged in response to what she'd said, but it wasn't off-putting. Just a way to protect himself from the risk of peeling back the scar to finally allow the wound to heal. She should know. She'd barely worked through the worst of it, and a lot of that had been under protest because the people in her family hadn't allowed her to suffer.

Catalina's phone rang, loud enough she winced and

hopped up out of the chair. The young woman across the circle grinned.

Cat said, "Busted. Sorry, guys."

She pulled out her phone and silenced it but left it to ring. Why was Romeo calling her while he was on shift?

Her whole body stiffened, and a hundred things raced through her mind. Horrible scenarios. One or both of her parents. Her brother.

"Everything okay, Cat?" Rebecca asked.

"I should take this. Sorry to be rude." Cat swiped the screen, winding between her chair and Simon's. "Hello?" She rushed to the door so she could talk at a normal volume in the hallway. "Romeo, is everything okay?"

"It's fine, but it's not." He didn't sound hurt.

"Mom and Dad?"

"This isn't about them. It's about one of the students at your school. Lots of reports with your name on them. Marianna Barker? Her parents reported her missing tonight, and there are indications she was abducted." His voice lowered at the end, meaning he had to be in public. "The mom asked for you to come, or I wouldn't have called you."

"You should have, regardless." After all, she could provide insight to the investigating detectives.

"Cat—"

Fire burned in her abdomen. "Text me the address. I'm on my way."

Her brother didn't think she had any business being a cop any more than the rest of them did. She'd been shot in the line of duty.

Exactly what else did she have left to prove?

EIGHT

The group pretty much wrapped up after Cat left to take her call. She'd looked so worried he skipped out on talking to Rebecca—even though she looked like she wanted to talk to him. He'd already had her sign his paper when he arrived. Maybe this could be as painless as possible.

Then again, the name of the game was trauma recovery.

Cat had shared about her injury, and the pain he'd seen on her face was more than just physical. She grieved. He saw the same look in his sister's eyes when she didn't think anyone was looking—usually on the anniversary of their mother's death.

Simon stepped out into the hall and found her pacing. He'd stopped for a second and heard her say she would be there soon. Whatever it was didn't look good. He walked near to her before she could rush off. "Everything okay?"

"No, *Simon*. It's not okay."

Yeah, so he deserved that one. "I wasn't going to tell you my real name when it wasn't necessary for you to know."

She wouldn't have recognized it, most likely. Though it was possible since his father had been a local criminal involved in trafficking until he was killed not even two years ago. His sister had been a local EMT, and his brother-in-law was a detective in homicide, or major crimes, or whatever they called it. Their family was intricately connected to Vanguard.

And why did the idea she might have an opinion about him or his family make him nervous? Simon needed the chance to prove to her he was a good guy, not a disaster who cried at hearing about a cop who got shot.

"What's going on, Cat?"

She frowned and looked as if she was going to ask him to call her Officer Alvarez. Instead, she said, "One of the female students at the school has gone missing. It's a possible abduction." She looked at her phone. "I'm going to go talk to the mom."

Simon nodded. "I'll go with you."

He could ride with her in her car, and they could talk. He could explain more about giving her a fake name, and even though his back was way up against the wall on this one, it would give him a chance to do what Rebecca said. Find some good in the situation.

Cat was like a beacon in the night.

A hero, shot in the line of duty. Now, she worked with teens, keeping the next generation safe. What wasn't to like about this intriguing, fiery woman who was not at all pleased with him right now?

She only frowned deeper. "Why do you want to come?"

"I might be able to help."

She glanced at him, then turned and walked to the front doors. His bike was parked beside the entrance in a spot meant for bicycles, but in this neighborhood, no way was he leaving a nice motorcycle in the parking lot with too many dark shadows between streetlights.

She stepped off the curb onto the asphalt. "Are you going to ride with me? I can bring you back for your bike later."

"Sure." He didn't even know which gray compact was hers. Simon turned to his bike. Did he really want to leave it?

"Come on." She headed into the parking lot, weaving between cars.

He jogged to catch up, adjusting his backpack on his shoulders as he ran. At the car, he touched the handle and immediately felt a shiver down his back. The same as he'd felt outside the hotel.

Had that been because some part of his awareness knew Jasper was in the room before his conscious mind became aware of it? Maybe he'd seen a familiar car in the lot but hadn't placed it. Or he had spotted movement in the window and not registered it.

"Okay?"

"I don't ride in cars much."

Cat stared at him over the roof. "You can ride your bike and follow me."

And both of them would know he'd done it because he couldn't stomach being in a car. "No." He cleared his throat. "I'm good."

Simon pulled the door open and slid in. He spotted the other group members heading out of the community center building. Lonely, wounded souls that made him think of tragic country songs. Nothing he would ever listen to. When he did listen to music, it was a classical mix that didn't detract from his thoughts and, in fact, actually helped him focus on whatever problem he was trying to solve.

He hadn't listened to music in a while.

Not since...

Simon shook his head and buckled up in time for Cat to

pull onto the road. "So you know this girl, or she just goes to the school? I don't know the protocol with SROs."

He could text his brother-in-law and find out, but just like Peter, his sister, Freya, and her husband, Lucas, both thought he was backpacking in Yellowstone National Park.

"I've met with Marianna a few times. She was on my radar of kids worth checking on." Cat drove with an easy grace, not too crazy like his sister. Freya drove like her butt was on fire, which Peter said helped with his defensive driving training course since she'd taught them both how to drive.

The ache in his chest caused by thinking of his family wasn't unusual, but it caught him off guard now, nonetheless.

He rubbed the heel of his hand across his chest.

His phone buzzed. He turned it over and looked at the new message.

"Who is Talia?"

He glanced at Cat. "Huh?"

"Sorry." She winced. "I saw her name on your phone earlier. Thought she might be someone…"

Like a girlfriend? What did it mean that she'd wondered that?

He said, "Talia's married. Her husband is a Secret Service agent. I work at Vanguard and that guy scares me, so that's saying something about how huge he is. He would bury me in some frozen part of Canada, and no one would ever see me again. But that's not the point. Talia is great. She's an NSA agent on a counter-terrorism taskforce, and we bounce ideas back and forth. Mostly math equations. We wrote our own app like Wordle and send each other challenges every day."

He hadn't even checked it this morning.

Simon said, "They have three kids. Talia is great. She'll call you 'honey' and 'child' and read you the riot act while she's looking at more gold purses online, finding a deal with some obscure coupon, and buying them for herself for some occasion she just made up."

Cat chuckled. "I have a cousin like that. She scares me, but at the same time I also want to be her."

Simon had to laugh with her. "So you feel my pain."

She glanced over. Words escaped him. Maybe they did understand each other. Could it be true? Cat Alvarez was the kind of woman he'd be able to trust. History didn't have any bearing on how she would treat him. He wouldn't jump in with no clue what he was in for, but she intrigued him in a completely unexpected way.

He typed a reply to Talia about the communication network and all the messages they'd found earlier before he had to leave. He wasn't about to tell her about Jasper's ridiculous ultimatum, so he hadn't shared where he was. From what they'd discovered, there was something locally being passed around the network. Some kind of signal that something was going down tonight.

Instead of wondering what on earth that was, he'd much rather be doing something good with a woman like Cat. Helping the community.

Almost felt as good as seeing a student suddenly grasp a concept that had eluded them before he explained it.

Fifteen minutes later, she pulled onto a street lined with police cars. Flashing lights. People gathered around. Cat parked and reached over for the glove compartment. She drew out a badge and a holstered gun, sliding both on her belt as he walked beside her to the source of all the attention. Simon had his backpack, just in case.

He scanned the crowd for familiar faces, hoping he saw none but, at the same time, hoping people he trusted were working this.

The officer on the tape recognized Cat. "Alvarez."

"Hey, Paul. Romeo here?"

"Sis!"

Simon glanced beyond the tape to see a uniformed officer walking toward them. The guy said, "She's with me. Let her in."

Cat thumbed in Simon's direction. "He's with me?" The doubt in her voice made it sound like a question.

"Tech support from Vanguard. If needed." Simon didn't have anything else to offer. Just the one thing that made him valuable to the company he worked for. And the bad guys they were always trying to take down.

He glanced back over his shoulder but saw no one that made him want to run away screaming in terror. Romeo Alvarez was a stocky guy the same height as his sister. They'd met a couple of times.

Romeo nodded, not hiding his confusion at the fact Simon was with his sister. "Simon Olson."

Cat said, "I guess I'm the last to know." She kissed her brother's cheek and moved around him. "I'll be inside."

Simon watched her go, careful to keep his face impassive. Before Romeo could ask, Simon said, "I'm working a job at the school. Nothing to do with Cat, and she won't be in any danger."

"You can't possibly guarantee that nothing will happen to her."

Simon shrugged. "Maybe not, but I can tell you that the scope of what I'm doing goes nowhere near her."

"Then maybe you should follow suit."

"You know, I'm gonna go inside. See if they need any tech help." He walked by Romeo, half expecting the guy to pull some tough guy move like shoulder-checking him.

Simon headed down the front walk, cracked concrete

flanked by bare, dry grass. Kids' scooter. One beat-up running shoe that looked like a dog had chewed it.

To the front steps, where the door swung open before he even got there.

His brother-in-law, Lucas Westbrook, stomped off the step and came right up to him. Way too close. "Backpacking? Now I find out you're here?"

Simon winced inwardly. He wasn't going to back down, but that didn't mean he wasn't quaking in his shoes. "I can explain."

"And you're gonna. Just as soon as a scared-out-of-her-mind teenage girl has been returned to her scared-out-of-their-minds family and I have a second to think. Got it?"

Simon nodded, clenching his teeth so hard his jaw hurt.

"Everything okay?" Cat stood in the doorway.

"Just welcoming my brother back from his trip." Lucas spun on his heels and stomped back into the house.

Simon blew out a long breath. He wouldn't be surprised if Freya and Peter were in the hotel room when he got back tonight. Maybe he needed to get a new one. But all that would do was prolong the inevitable reckoning. Might as well get it over with, the way he'd just done with Lucas.

Cat said, "I know brothers. That wasn't good."

"Be grateful you only have one." Simon wasn't looking forward to any of it. "Freya will be worse, though."

"That's Lucas's wife, right?"

"You know them?"

Cat shrugged a shoulder. "I need to speak with the mother. She's pretty upset."

He nodded. "I won't keep you. I can do a lot just from my laptop, and anything I find will go to the police."

The look she gave him spoke to her trust in him. Now more than before—a lot more, all because of his association to cops. But he would take it. Whatever endeared him to her, he would claim it.

"Thanks for coming with me."

Simon nodded. "You're welcome."

Between her brother and his family, it felt like a tiny bubble of something good in the middle of everything swirling around him. Which reminded him of what the group leader had said. Maybe in order to find something good, he just had to look for it.

It had to be a sign he was exactly where he was supposed to be.

Which meant taking the job at the school had been the right thing.

Now he just had to finish it.

NINE

Despite all the ways it wasn't a good idea, Cat couldn't let go of the realization that Simon's family dynamic was pretty similar to hers. She stepped inside the house with Romeo right behind her, trying to figure out how she was going to keep her distance when the guy became more and more human every moment she spent in his presence.

"You okay?"

She glanced aside at Romeo. "Yeah, actually. I think I am."

Her ex, Pastor Tyler Cunningham, had presented himself as superhuman. A hero. A star. She'd been swept along by it, suckered in. Effectively starstruck, even though he was a local guy with a local following. To be the center of his attention—or so she'd thought—had been hypnotic.

Until she discovered the giant fissure underneath where his character should've been. Honesty. Integrity. Sincerity. It had all been absent.

Romeo glanced back, probably at Simon.

Cat asked, "Are you going to tell me to stay away because he's bad news?" Although his real name had come out, that wasn't much information, so maybe there was something she should know. Some gaping issue or a red flag.

Romeo made a face. "Believe me, I would if I could."

Inside, the entryway preceded a hall lined with older pine wood flooring. The single-story house had three bedrooms, and the kitchen was to the right past the living room. The bedrooms to the left.

Detectives stood in the living room, one of them Simon's brother-in-law. Marianna's mother, Leanna, sat in an armchair with her legs bent so her feet were on the seat, her arms around her knees. She was barely thirty-five but looked much older tonight.

Cat heard a shuffle and peeked down the hall. Marianna's little sister stood in her bedroom doorway, clutching a blanket with her thumb in her mouth.

Cat took a couple of steps, crouched, and waved the girl over.

Bridget scurried to stand in front of her, maybe five years old. Old enough to have grown out of the stage where she needed a blanket for comfort, but young enough still that she went back to it on a night like tonight.

"You okay, Bridge?"

The little girl sniffed. Her eyes were hollow. She took the last couple of steps toward Cat and climbed up on her knee. *Ouch.* Not her good leg. Cat slid her arms under the girl and tried to figure out how to stand and keep hold of her without them both going down.

She adjusted the girl's weight to her left hip rather than on her weapon side and planted her left foot so she could— hopefully—rise without falling.

Halfway up, she faltered. Someone grasped her elbow, holding her steady. She leaned into it and looked over to find Simon slightly behind her left shoulder. "Thanks."

She held the girl to her front.

He only nodded. A second later, he was back to looking at the screen of his laptop.

Cat wasn't going to watch him work when a room full of people were looking at her—one of them his sister's husband. She headed for the living room and settled onto the couch, not letting go of Bridget. The little girl sighed against her, every inhale a choppy breath.

The middle sister hadn't appeared. Cat asked, "Where's Marge?"

Leanna stared blankly at the coffee table and the stack of magazines about famous people and weird medical conditions.

Bridget said, "Crying in the bathtub."

One of the detectives, not Simon's brother, said, "I'll get a female officer to check on her." He walked by Romeo, who hung back nearly in the hall, and walked out.

Lucas caught Cat's eye and motioned with a tip of his head to the missing girl's mom. Apparently, they wanted her to try talking to the woman.

She shifted on the couch. "Leanna? Can you tell me what happened?"

After a second with no response, when Cat was almost about to nudge the woman, she turned her head and looked at Cat.

"Tell me what happened." She kept her voice soft in case the worried mother got spooked.

"She came home from work." Leanna sniffed.

"Her car is here?"

Leanna nodded, dropping her cheek to her knee with her face angled toward Cat. "The yellow Nissan."

Romeo left the room.

"So, she came home..." Cat let that drift off, inviting Leanna to keep talking.

"I heard her car. She came down the side, to the kitchen door. I was watching TV. When I heard the kitchen door open, I yelled for her to take the trash out before she took her shoes off."

Cat asked, "Did she respond?"

Leanna shook her head. "She doesn't normally. Unless she's arguing. So, I figured she did it."

"And then?"

Leanna winced. "She never came back in. I went to check, and she was nowhere. Not in her room. Not outside in the alley where the trash cans are. She was just gone."

A sinking feeling descended in Cat's stomach, but at the same time, she had a lot of questions. Why this girl? Why here, tonight? There had to be easier places to snatch her if that was even what had happened.

It wasn't her case, but that didn't absolve her from caring. *Lord, help her. Wherever she is, don't let her be scared. Protect her heart. Her mind. Her body.*

Cat shuddered. *We need peace, Lord.* For a second, she felt better, but reality seemed stronger than the tiny flicker of faith inside her.

She pulled her thoughts back to the situation, trying to think of it more like a case than a missing person she knew and cared about. "Leanna, how has she seemed lately?"

The mom sniffed again and lifted her head. "What do you mean?"

"Like her mood. Has she seemed happy or stressed about anything?"

Leanna frowned. "She's still always on her phone. That's nothing different, but it seemed like something on there was upsetting her. I asked her what was going on, but she told me not to worry about it."

"Do you think maybe someone was giving her a hard time? Did she have any problems with friends?" The little girl leaning against Cat's side let out a long breath, as if she had fallen asleep. Cat needed to stretch out her leg but didn't want to disturb Bridget.

"I don't know. I should've asked her. I should've—" Her voice broke.

"You didn't know this would happen. It isn't your fault." She glanced at Lucas. "What about her phone?"

The detective shook his head. "We're looking for it."

Cat turned back to Leanna. "What about a laptop? Does Marianna have one?"

"We couldn't afford to buy one. The one she used at school she gave back at the end of the year."

"And she's not enrolled in summer school?" Cat hadn't seen her there.

Leanna shook her head. "She's been working a lot, trying to save up."

"What is she going to do with the money?"

"Get out of here. That's all she said. Go to college somewhere else."

Trying to escape the place you grew up was a pretty normal teenage dream. Cat didn't read anything into that simple desire, though it could absolutely be indicative of a problem Marianna needed to run from.

Who—or what—did she want to escape?

"Where does she work?" Cat hadn't heard about the job that she must've gotten in the past few months, since the last time they talked. Marianna hadn't been working earlier this year.

"The burger place on Central, past the library."

"Thanks, Leanna."

"Are you going to find her?"

Cat couldn't promise they would. All she could say was, "We're going to do everything we can."

Commotion erupted in the hall. A door slammed open, and someone called for a medic. One cop ran toward the door and yelled, "Medic now!"

The cop and two EMTs ran the other way seconds later, heading down the hall. Bridget stirred against her. Cat shifted enough to lay the girl on the couch and tugged a blanket from the back of the couch onto her. Leanna didn't move, and that blank stare hadn't left her face.

Cat went into the hall in time to see one of the EMTs carrying a young girl in his arms, wrapped in a huge towel. Nearly gray. Blood soaked the front of the towel. They rushed past her, but the officer stopped in the hall.

"What happened, Sergeant?"

The female cop wasn't one Cat knew. Older than Cat, with chevrons on her sleeves, the cop had her dark blonde hair pulled back and a shadowed look in her eyes. "Slit her wrists. Got deep on the left side but didn't cut much on the right. She'd already passed out before I got in there."

"I'm glad you found her in time."

The sergeant nodded and went outside.

Detective Westbrook moved to stand with her. "You think it's worth asking the mom more questions, Officer Alvarez?"

Was this a test? Probably not. It was her father who asked those types of questions. "Not now, but I'd try again later. Or in the morning if Marianna is still missing." She spoke quietly, praying the distraught mom didn't overhear.

Lucas nodded.

"All the stats about abductions are running through my mind. Is that normal?"

His expression softened, and he stuck a hand in his slacks pocket. "Yes, which is when you know it's time to regroup, find out what everyone has, and make a plan for what to do next." He lifted his chin, indicating down the hall. "Which also means we need to find Simon."

She started off toward the bedrooms. "What was he working on?"

"Who knows with that kid." Lucas's tone warmed, and it sounded endearing. "The guy is a genius. There's nothing he can't hack or figure out on a computer. I heard the NSA was trying to recruit him a few months ago."

"But he didn't take the job?" She stopped at Marianna's room. A profusion of purple spread all over the room, and the letters of her name stretched over the mirror, stuck there like flags on a string. A teen room with leftover items from her childhood bedroom.

Lucas frowned. "I actually...don't know what happened. I heard there was a meeting, but nothing after that." He paused. "Simon doesn't talk much about what's going on in his head or what he's working on. I guess I assumed if things weren't okay, he would say something. But maybe I shouldn't have."

Who would Simon confide in? His family, or his twin brother? Maybe he had confided in this Talia friend of his? Hopefully, he had someone to talk to.

Seemed like maybe the same thing had happened with Marianna. It was definitely easier to assume the people Cat cared for were fine and that they'd say something if they weren't. She needed to check in with her parents and make sure she wasn't wrong about that assumption.

Cat looked around the room, trying to see through the surface to what secrets the girl had kept underneath. Who would she talk to if she were having problems with someone? A best friend, most likely. They'd need to find who that was, maybe by talking to her work friends.

"Hey." Lucas glanced down the hall, and she heard footsteps approaching.

Simon appeared beside him and jerked his head to flip hair back from his face. "I found her phone."

TEN

They followed him to the kitchen door and then outside to where the signal originated. Simon stood back. "In the trash can."

Lucas asked, "You're sure?"

Simon nodded. "That's the source of the signal."

Even if it wasn't Marianna's phone, it was someone's. Found via a regular commercial network, so not connected to the communication network he'd created—which was a seriously good note to be able to make. The last thing he needed was for the two cases to collide. This was a normal missing teen case. No broader connection.

He squared his shoulders while Lucas dug around in the trash can. A uniformed cop brought over a tarp, and they spread out the garbage, tearing open bags and looking inside. The phone had ended up under a white plastic bag, stretched out by the contents. "Got it."

Lucas stood with the phone in his gloved hand.

Simon was aware of Cat beside him, her attention partially on him. She had a way of tuning in to the body language of others, and she could probably tell he still hadn't quite found his equilibrium after the meeting. Then they'd come here, and he'd had to confront Lucas.

His family knew that he'd lied about his vacation.

Simon's phone had been silent. Whether or not Lucas had sent texts to Freya and Peter, they would find out soon enough, and then he'd be in for a reckoning.

Silence was worse than a confrontation.

Alone was worse than with people, and quiet was worse than a room full of chatter. He would much rather be with people than on his own. Like this, where he was working and helping, but the real responsibility fell on the cops here.

His father might've said that meant he didn't measure up, but the support role Simon had in his life suited him. Not an operator. Not a team leader, or someone who went out and kicked doors down. Simon was the one who backed up those people. This was his calling. His mission. The work he was supposed to do.

Like helping teens figure out complex math problems. As if what he had chosen to do made a difference, and he could keep his quiet role in the meantime. Not the center of attention. Not the one who got all the praise. That was the last thing he wanted.

Simon's peace of mind was more valuable to him than all of that. Like the grasp he had on his freedom, and the ability to choose for himself where he went. What he did.

He needed those things like he needed air.

To not feel trapped.

Captive.

"Bro."

Oh, Lucas was talking to him. "What's that?"

"We need to go ask the mom for permission. If she gives it, can you get into the phone? It'll go a whole lot faster than if we pass it to the department tech. We can get the paperwork done later so you're listed as a contractor for this case."

Simon nodded. "I just need a cable from my backpack."

Lucas said, "Let's go ask."

They all trailed back inside, down the hall. He waited in the entryway with Cat while Lucas talked to the mom.

A second later, he heard a frustrated, "Just do it. Find her."

Lucas got up and came back to them. A female officer moved to crouch by Leanna Barker, speaking to her quietly.

His brother-in-law nudged him. "Outside."

Simon went to the corner of the grass by the front door, just off the step where he'd stashed his backpack. Cat stood on the sidewalk nearby. Romeo Alvarez had one eye on him, the other on the uniformed officer he was talking to. The eagle eye wasn't something he appreciated, but as a guy with a sister, Simon at least understood where he was coming from.

The friendship with Cat was way too new for anyone to think anything about what might become of it. He'd heard some of her story, and if she told him more, he'd listen to what she experienced in the shooting when she was a beat cop. The kind of time spent with someone where you talked until the wee hours about all kinds of things.

The way he used to do with Peter, as kids. Side by side in twin beds. Turned toward each other so they could whisper, and dad wouldn't hear them talking.

He loved to get to know people in the quiet. When his ex-girlfriend hadn't ever wanted to sit on his balcony and just talk, he should've realized the relationship was doomed. He'd ignored the signs it wouldn't last and wound up getting his heart stomped on.

Simon plugged one end of the cord into his laptop, the other end had a plastic circle disk on it.

"How does this work?" Cat sounded interested.

He took the phone in its plastic evidence bag and motioned to the grass. "Come here, I'll show you." He sat on the grass and crossed his legs, then placed the laptop on the grass. "Set the phone on that disk. You don't have to take it out of the bag. It'll connect wirelessly to the computer."

Cat settled beside him, sitting close enough that she could lean against his shoulder. "I thought you'd have to plug it in."

Simon leaned forward and typed on the computer keyboard. "See here. It's connected." He pointed at the screen, aware of the slight dampness of the grass under him. Good thing he didn't need to impress a woman right now because he might look like he'd sat in something when he got up.

Beside him, Cat peered at the screen. Apparently, she didn't care about sitting on the grass either.

The warm night felt good on his skin. He scrubbed the back of his neck, and the long hair that probably could use cutting. Why did he have the burning desire to ask her if she liked guys with hair long enough that they could tie it back or if she preferred hair like Peter's, short like an operator?

He typed as he thought, doing both at the same time since manipulating the computer was second nature for him, like driving and suddenly realizing you'd been deep in thought and didn't remember how you got there.

Tonight had been rough in a lot of ways, but maybe things would get better now that Lucas knew.

They could find this missing teen.

Everything would go back to normal. Simon would solve his own problem without them needing to worry about him. After all, they could see for themselves he was fine.

At the edge of his awareness, he could hear people talking. Onlookers and cops. Maybe a news reporter.

He hit Enter. "Here we go." Windows populated on the screen, tabs with social media sites and other accounts. "Everything she's logged into on her phone, we'll get access to it. Not all of it is relevant."

She leaned against his shoulder. "But you never know what might be."

Simon nodded, hyperaware of her closeness. It felt like companionship and support—neither of which he'd been expecting this week. He'd been determined to go it alone. Keep apart from anyone who could be hurt by what he did.

Drawing attention to himself never went well, and with this investigation, someone could die.

"Talked to the neighbors." Romeo strode up to him. Probably, this guy and Peter would be good friends—if they weren't already.

Cat asked, "Anything?"

"No one has a doorbell cam with a view of this house. An older lady might've seen a cable van, a contractor, not the company vehicle. I'll follow up with them, but the timing isn't quite right." Romeo lifted his chin. "You found her phone?"

"Simon did." Cat almost sounded impressed.

All he'd done was track each of the signals connected to the Wi-Fi in the house.

Simon clicked through the open windows. One was a social media site with direct messaging. He winced at the contents of the first one that popped up—fourteen new messages. A group thread with a number of different people, all of whom seemed to have targeted Marianna with their ire. "She was being harassed."

He sent the access information to Lucas's PD email address. The detective could pass it to their tech department to comb through.

Simon found the window with Marianna's text messages.

One of the numbers said *Hidden Sender*, and the thread seemed pretty one-sided. Once in a while, the teen had replied.

> Leave me alone.

He knew what that felt like.

Simon rolled his shoulders and clicked to see the number. Nothing but an IP address to indicate the source of the messages. He frowned. It couldn't be... He gritted his teeth and did a quick copy and paste into the other program.

Talia would notice. He'd promised to share all the intel with her, which probably meant her boss knew all about what they were doing. He should tell Lucas and Peter that when they got all worked up about him being alone. He had help. If anything had happened to him, Talia would've told them right away.

Ping.

"What does that mean?"

Simon's stomach flipped over.

Cat touched his arm. "Sie, what does that mean?"

Her voice warped and echoed around him while his ears did that weird thing where he disconnected. He pushed back against it, anchoring himself in the here and now. The ground. Warm night air on the skin of his arms. Cat sitting close by him, and the fact she cared about people.

"Something else." He blew out a breath and quickly sent everything from the phone to Lucas's email. Then he closed the lid of the laptop and stood. He shoved it into his backpack, and the corner caught. He swiped the laptop off the grass and got it in fine on the second try.

"Bro—"

He shook his head. "I have to go."

"Suddenly, at ten o'clock at night?" Lucas walked over. "What happened? What did you just see on her phone?"

How could he explain it?

Cat stood as well. "Text messages from someone. A hidden number."

Lucas stared at him. "Who was she talking to?"

"I don't know whose phone it was."

"But you're gonna go find out?"

Cat gasped, turning to him. One hand touched his arm. "Sie, are you saying she's connected to your case at the school?"

His last meal threatened a reappearance. He sucked in a breath through his nose. "I don't..." His thoughts fragmented. "I need to figure it out. I can't do that here."

His breath was coming fast. The world seemed to spin around him.

Cat said something he didn't register.

Lucas shifted too close. "I'm calling Peter."

"No!" Simon whipped around to him. "I don't want him here!"

He backed up a couple of steps, stumbling on the uneven grass. *Get it together.* But no matter what he said to himself, that same fear he'd tried to stuff down was now swallowing him whole.

He needed to get out of here.

Simon glanced around. Anywhere was better than here where far too many people were looking at him. *Escape like you did last time.*

Cat moved in front of him. "Simon, look at me."

He managed to still enough to focus on her face.

She stretched out her arm. "Take my hand."

"I have to go."

She motioned with her hand. "I'll drive." She stepped a fraction closer. "Whatever you're scared of—"

"I'm not scared." Why would anyone believe that? He didn't, but who wanted to be the victim?

"Whatever, whoever it is, they're not here. Who is here?" Cat asked, but she wasn't looking for a response. "A whole lot of people who aren't going to let anything happen to you."

"I have to go." Somewhere. Anywhere that he wouldn't have to pretend to be strong.

She took his hand. "So let's go."

ELEVEN

"I'm not weak."

Simon strode ahead of her into her house. He hadn't said much on the drive over, and she didn't try to coax anything out of him. His reaction had been unexpected but not out of the ordinary. It seemed as if no one who knew him understood. Which meant he hadn't told them the story.

He'd been keeping it in all this time.

No wonder it hit him hard.

"Let's get a soda and sit."

Simon turned to her, standing by her kitchen table. He looked lost. But she wasn't the one who would find him. She walked over and flipped off the light he'd turned on when he walked into her house.

Cat touched his arm as she passed. He didn't react at all. She blinked at the light in the fridge and got two cans, one a cola and the other a clear soda. "Come on."

She waited in the doorway, and he followed tentatively. Still in shock. Or knowing she would likely get him to talk about what happened to him as soon as they sat. She ran her hand down his arm, tugging on his hand. "Here."

Hopefully, he would find it easier in the dark.

She set his hand on the back of the chair and offered him his choice of drink flavor. She heard him ease into the chair, and the can popped. She hit the button on the remote, and the blinds on the floor-to-ceiling windows rose slowly. The muted yellow of streetlights below them gave the room a mustard tint.

"Whoa."

"It's why I bought this condo." Here on the east side of town, she'd grabbed up a place with a view out the back that was nothing but mountains. Trees. Lots of the residents skied out the back door of the building, taking a lift from the edge of the property to the top of the mountain. This time of year, it was hiking trails, miles of open space to explore.

Right now, the night sky stretched above the peaks with an ocean of stars.

Cat settled into the chair to the left, both armchairs facing the windows. She curled her legs up and took a long draw from the soda. Her bookcase to the left overflowed with all her favorites, shelves of books she'd bought but hadn't read yet. She still continued to purchase them, making space in her life for more of what she loved.

"It's beautiful."

"It's calming, even with you here. Romeo fidgets nonstop." She chuckled just a little, pulling the cushion from under her elbow to hold it on her lap. "He never could sit still as a kid."

"Peter and I were like that. Used to drive my mother crazy trying to do school with us. Freya would be in the corner, reading."

"What happened?"

"My mother was killed when we were in middle school.

My father brought us home to Benson, and we went to school. He continued his criminal empire here until Freya and Lucas took him down."

Cat let the words dissipate in the air, giving him a moment with the comfort of silence. The peace that quiet could bring. "What happened?"

She heard a slurp, and a second later a long sigh. "I don't like being weak."

"Fear isn't weakness." Trauma didn't always mean fear, and a lot of the time, it wasn't something a person could control. "It's about acknowledging there are things you can't control. When it overwhelms me, I sit here. Where I remember I can find peace with the God who made the stars and the mountains. The One who is so much more powerful than my fear."

"God is...well, He's God, but that whole thing is twisted around in my head. Maybe there are a lot of things twisted around in there."

If anyone understood that, it was Cat. "For a long time, I asked God why my partner died and I lived. Why did a man who was beloved—a father, a husband—lose his life and I survived?"

She heard him shift in the chair.

Cat said, "It was a convenience store robbery. The kid was clearly in over his head, but it could've turned into a hostage situation had we not gone in. We saved everyone inside. *He* saved them." She cleared her throat. "He was my training officer, Sergeant Ellis. I was three weeks out of the academy, and I haven't been back on a beat since."

"You switched to being an SRO after the shooting?"

Cat nodded but he likely couldn't see it with no light except what filtered in from outside. "I didn't even try. I just quit that kind of policing and took another assignment. So, I understand thinking that your fear makes you weak. I thought that for a long time, but I like what I do now. I make a difference in the school."

"You're right about that."

It warmed her to know he thought so. "I've come a long way. It hasn't always been easy, but nothing worth it is supposed to be easy."

"Well, burying my head in the sand and pretending it wasn't a problem didn't work for me." He huffed out a breath that was probably supposed to be a laugh. "So, I decided to disconnect from everything and everyone and solve it myself."

"Sounds familiar." She sipped her drink. "I've been trying to settle on who it was that shot me ever since it happened."

"But the shooter was convicted, wasn't he?"

She said, "I don't believe he was telling the truth. I think he was coerced into a confession."

"I'll help if I can."

"Thanks." She ran a hand over her knee. "Do you think Marianna's disappearance is connected to the job you're doing at the school?"

"I would've said no, but her phone received harassing messages from a phone on the communication network I'm trying to dismantle."

And somehow, that tied to a traumatic experience for him? "That's the job? Taking down a network?"

"It's a communications platform. Any phone can be wiped and added to it, so I don't know how big it is now. Everyone connects to it over Wi-Fi rather than a phone signal from a tower, but if there's no Wi-Fi, they can connect to a satellite. If I can get to the central server where the program is running, I can shut it down. But I have to find out where it's being hosted."

"You really are good at this computer stuff, aren't you?"

She could get around on her laptop and do some things beyond just the basics. She'd set up the connection with her new printer all by herself after her last printer quit.

"I wrote the program for the network." His voice thickened as he spoke.

That was it. There it was. The source of his stress reaction. "I'd like to know what happened to you, if you feel comfortable sharing."

Silence filled the room for a time. Minutes. Then several minutes.

"We were seventeen. Freya was at work. It was a Thursday. I remember that. I had a math test the next day, and I ended up failing that class. Peter hadn't finished his chores, and I wanted to go out. So I walked to the gas station for a soda." He cleared his throat. "Halfway back, a car pulled over. I ran, but two guys tackled me. They shoved a hood over my head and tossed me in the car."

Cat winced.

"I remember it being too hot. Too close. People all around me, all the time. I think I hit my head because I remember throwing up a few times. Then I was in a shower with a lot of bruises. It was freezing. I slept on a cold floor. I never saw their faces, but they kept me in a basement."

He cleared his throat. "A couple of days later, he came. I got the hood again. He left pictures of my family and told me he had a job for me. If I didn't do it, he would kill my sister and my brother. Maybe he knew my dad and maybe he didn't. I just remember I was way more afraid of him than I'd ever been of my father."

Cat blinked back the tears that pricked at her eyes.

"Someone had started the program. They didn't get far before they ran into a snag. I don't know who it was or what happened to them." He sucked in a choppy breath. "I fixed it and finished the job. I had the connection I'd need to contact someone and ask for help, but I didn't know who to ask. We were already working for Vanguard then, but I didn't trust them enough. I didn't know what I know now, and I'm going to regret not reaching out for the rest of my life."

He wasn't being fair to himself.

Before she could tell him that, he continued, "They weren't going to let me go. Things were going...badly. The boss was gone, and one of the guys..." He paused. "It was bad, and I knew I had to get out before something more horrible than all of it happened."

Cat bit her lip, scared for what was coming.

"He came in one night. I was almost taller than him but way too skinny. He was—he was going to touch me. Force me at gunpoint to..." Simon cleared his throat. "I flipped out. Next thing I knew, the gun was in my hand. It goes off, and his brains are all over the wall. So I ran. I was somewhere in central Washington at this family estate, but I can't figure out where I was exactly."

"You tried to find it?"

He said, "I've checked the family's property holdings, but there's no property in that general area listed anywhere under their name. I just ran. I don't have any reference for where I was. Also, I don't know which family member it was that held me because I never saw them. I got home and told everyone I'd been sick. I looked awful, so it wasn't a stretch."

"You never told anyone?"

"Maybe Peter knows. He probably does. But he chooses to ignore it, and he'll do that until I force him to confront it. Which I never have." Simon sighed. "He's still out there. The boss. Sometimes, it feels like he's watching me. It's why I've never left Benson. I don't want to go on missions. I just want to work in the office."

"I feel that way about police work, and no one understands it but me." Cat sniffed. "And now you."

The idea that he got her in a way no one else did settled in her heart. She wanted to keep hold of it and nurture it like a precious thing.

Cat asked, "How do you know the communication network connects to the school?"

"One of the kids. I saw a picture in the house where I was held, but he was little at the time. It was actually a Little League team picture. I saw the kid's name, and I tracked him to the school when I was looking for a way to get to the server hosting site. I know he has one of the phones, so I'm using a connection to that to get directly into the network in a way that could give us the geographical location of the site. Talia is helping me. She knows what happened, and she went through a situation of her own. She understands the fear." He let out a breathy exhale. "I thought I was doing okay."

"I'm sure you were. Trauma is a tricky beast. You can be fine and then suddenly..."

"You're not." He sighed. "Maybe it was the texts. Knowing she was backed into a corner, harassed, and now she's been taken."

"So help me find her, and I'll help you fix your problem. Take this network down."

"You really want to team up?"

If she turned on a light so he could see her face, then he'd have his answer. "I want another soda. We can talk about something dumb, like stupid movies we loved. Music. I'm praying right now that you like to read books because that might be a deal breaker."

"And the case?"

Cat said, "By tomorrow, the police will have more information. Right now, I can pray for Marianna, but there's not much else I can do. The department has it handled. If we let them work and we rest up, when they get fatigued, we can pitch in."

"All right."

Cat smiled to herself. "I'll get us more soda."

"I got it." He levered himself to the edge of the chair but didn't get up. "Thanks, Cat."

She looked at him, even if he couldn't see it. "You did absolutely the right thing shooting that guy. You have nothing to regret. You were strong enough to have survived, and that makes you amazing."

He had escaped.

She had crawled across a floor to watch her partner die.

They weren't equals or in competition, but one day, she hoped to find her shooter.

Then she might be able to think the same about herself.

TWELVE

Simon blinked awake, aware he was not alone.

Sunlight lit the floor in front of him, and his legs stretched out in front of the armchairs where he and Cat had talked long into the night. In the end, they'd been laughing and cracking jokes like old friends. Even with how the evening had started, it still ended well.

He looked over at the other chair, expecting to see Cat, but he blinked in surprise. It was his twin. "Pete."

Peter just sat there, watching him. If it was anyone else, he'd have been creeped out. But his twin had always been there with him in a way. Even when he was alone.

What had Peter thought of the time he'd been gone for a whole week? The shared emotions they sometimes experienced often left them overwhelmed. Had he told anyone that Simon might be in trouble? If so, then it hadn't amounted to anything. But Peter had to have felt something while Simon had been scared. Hurt.

When Simon had shown up back at home, Freya hadn't been happy with the fact he'd been missing. She hadn't gone to the police, though. Their father had barely noticed enough to care, and neither of them had pressed it with him. Until he told her he got sick, then she'd dropped the anger. Peter had given him a hug and said nothing.

Until now?

They didn't need to change how they were. It was the only thing in Simon's life he'd ever actually counted on, the fact he could rely on Peter. Though, he had to learn how to trust what he had with Vanguard. Slowly.

Simon shifted in the seat and looked out the window. The mountains looked better at night, like they had a bigger scale—more majestic somehow—but it was still a great view. Green landscape, trees, and jagged peaks. As if Catalina's backyard stretched for hundreds of miles.

This was a great place to sit.

She'd talked him down last night, brought him out of the fog he'd been in and settled him in a way no one else ever had. He could love her for that alone, but there was a whole lot more to her, and every layer she peeled back intrigued him further.

That didn't mean Simon was going to ask her to carry it all just so he could have what he wanted. It was too high of a price to ask her to pay for him to have the kind of relationship he'd always looked for. Never found. Thought he'd had but was sorely mistaken.

Now that he'd found a woman who could absolutely be "the one" for him, he couldn't ask her to share the load of baggage he hauled around.

Peter would tell him he should give it to God. Simon had avoided that entire subject for years.

"She believes." Peter would know what he meant. He always did, not like telepathy or anything. More like they were on the same wavelength. Same pattern of thinking. "You know I've been avoiding God."

Peter grunted. "Running as hard as you can in the opposite direction, trying to pretend you don't know the truth."

"Deep down. I know I can't deny it. That isn't it." Simon shifted on the chair. Someone had removed his shoes at some point, but he didn't know if it was Cat or Pete. "What time is it?"

"Just after five thirty."

And already so bright outside? "Did she let you in?"

Peter shook his head. As always, Simon saw shadows of their mother in his features. Or maybe Peter's presence simply made him remember. Good and bad. Ugly. Scars.

Her smile. The way she looked at him, as if he was special. All of it got mixed up in his head, like God's goodness and His wrath. The way their father twisted the Scriptures for his own ends, and there had been no objecting or questioning it without repercussions.

Some part of who God was felt a lot like that same authoritarian figure who had ruled them. And Simon had to contend with it. He had to wrestle God and find out what he needed to learn at the end.

"Probably feels like a train coming at you."

Simon asked, "You think I should admit defeat and surrender?"

"You don't quit or surrender. That's not how it works. You *yield*. To a better way than the path you've been on."

"You aren't going to let this go, are you?"

Peter made a huffing sound and only stared at him.

Simon sighed. Of course, he would have to face God. His brother had his head on straight about the Lord these days. He would get married soon. They would talk about having kids.

All that fear welled up in him again.

"Selena is worried about you. She was texting me all night to come and find you."

Better not to know how he had.

"Freya is worried. Even Clare called me about having a big meeting. Destiny told her that wasn't a good idea, they should let you keep going to the trauma group."

Simon said, "I don't need an intervention."

"When you do, you don't get a choice in it."

If anyone understood what he'd been through, it was Destiny. Given what had happened to her in Africa, she was probably the only one who did.

"I get why you don't want things to be public. I kept plenty to myself for a long time. But if it was me, would you let it go, or would you do everything you could to help me?"

Simon glanced over. "I already did that, remember?"

When Peter had been on that cruise, and his and Selena's lives had been in danger, Simon hadn't slept for three days while trying to find their ship. Trying to figure out what on earth was happening and get them help.

Pete nodded. A second later, he said, "I want all of it. Everything you've got on this case."

You're not my boss.

The corner of his brother's lips curled up, just a flash. "The disappearance of this girl is connected?"

Simon nodded. "No doubt."

"Okay." Peter sat forward on the chair, elbows on his knees.

"Hey, you're up." Cat's feet shuffled on the floor. "Oh, hey. Geez, you guys are twins, aren't you?" She leaned against the door, her soft expression just for him. "Coffee?"

He smiled. "Coffee would be great."

"None for me, thanks." Pete stood. "I should go. I just have a couple more questions."

So this was an interrogation. He glanced over at Pete. "Really?"

"Why is this a threat *now*? Suddenly, you drop off the grid and do this. Why the rush?"

Simon bristled. He'd already torn off that bandage for Cat, and his brother wanted him to recount the whole sordid thing all over again. Not just that, but how it had continued since. How it haunted him every minute of every day.

Peter asked, "He threatens you?"

Cat gasped. "He makes contact?"

Simon sat forward, scrubbed his hands down his face and then squeezed the back of his neck. He needed to—

"You're not running. Talk."

He winced. "Every so often, I get a message. A text."

"He is threatening you." Peter didn't ask it like a question, and he sounded like he wanted to find the man who had kidnapped Simon and kill him with his bare hands. Not something his brother should have on his conscience.

"I can handle it."

"Sie."

His brother really wanted to know? "You're getting married. You'll have kids one day. He'll come after you." Yet another way he was weak, not being strong enough to give up his family to keep them safe.

"So this *is* about my wedding."

Simon clenched his teeth.

"You said you were fine with it."

"Of course I'm fine with it! It's a good thing." Simon stood and paced to the window. Unbelievable that he had to reassure Pete this way.

"But you aren't going to be my best man?"

"You haven't asked me."

"It was a given."

"Then my answer is also a given."

Cat said, "I need coffee. This conversation is confusing."

Simon glanced at her for a second. Then he said to his brother, "I figured you'd ask me, so I was going to get this done before you set a date."

"Date's been set for months, bro. You've been ignoring that, too."

At least Pete didn't ask if it was about Lena. "I don't want you getting married if it's going to put you at risk."

"Life is always risky. Not much we can do about it, but we can choose to be happy when we find it."

And Simon was happy for him.

Pete glanced at the kitchen, then back at Simon. He came over and squeezed the back of Simon's neck, their abbreviated version of a hug. Simon wrapped his arm under Pete's and squeezed his shoulder from the back. They both let go.

"You never figured out where the threats were coming from?"

Simon shook his head. "Always from my network. But the kid is connected. I need to find the location where they host the server so I can shut it down for good."

"So we flip him. Get some answers."

Simon would've tried that if it had a guarantee. "We need a better plan than that."

Cat trailed back in with two cups of coffee. She handed one over to Simon. Peter intercepted it and took a swig. "Good stuff."

Simon took his cup from his brother. "You were leaving?"

Peter said, "There isn't just one girl missing. There are more."

Cat gasped.

"Sixteen-year-old local. Works at the movie theater, parents are on a two-week cruise. Pretty much checked out.

Her friends are all over social media looking for her, trying to figure out what happened. There's another, but it hasn't hit the police radar. Just the local news feeds."

Simon frowned. "This isn't your mission."

Peter said, "Go to work at the school today. Vanguard has your back."

"And I have no choice?"

Peter shrugged one shoulder. Everything about it was *you've got no choice.* "Quit fighting. It'll go easier."

"Why am I always the one who has to get with the program?"

Peter said, "No idea. But it's not that hard. You're not going to be hung out there alone for this one. And not ever again." He glanced at Cat. "Nice to meet you."

She lowered her mug. "Yeah, uh..."

Peter trailed out of the room.

"You, too."

The front door closed.

"Huh."

Simon started to chuckle.

"I don't think there's anything funny about that guy."

Simon laughed louder. She smiled. He tugged her to him, an arm around her shoulders. Careful not to jostle either of their mugs and make a spill. Simon kissed her forehead. "I don't know how he's gonna find the guy who had me abducted, but he will. And I almost feel bad for what's going to happen when Peter does catch up to him."

He winced. At least his brother would have the backing of Vanguard, no matter what happened.

She lifted up a little and planted a kiss on his cheek, a soft smile on her face. "He deserves worse than what your brother is going to do." Cat stepped back. "Breakfast? We'll have to have cereal, or we'll be late for school."

The comment caught him in nostalgia for a place he'd never been. "As long as we swing by the hotel so I can change out of yesterday's clothes."

"Sounds like a plan." She headed for the kitchen.

The promise in her voice warmed his heart.

As if they would be in this together. No matter what happened next.

THIRTEEN

Cat stared through the window at the class of attentive students, all watching Simon write on his tablet. Their eyes were trained on the screen behind him, transfixed until he reached a certain point. Several students erupted into cheers and at least one groaned.

"I knew it." One of the girls grinned at her friend.

Three seats down, Justice Spears stared at the girl with a hungry expression. Even for a hormonal teenage boy, this was just a little too predatory. But as soon as she registered it, the expression disappeared.

Cat shifted and rested the outside of her left arm against the metal of the locker, which was cold to the touch. The heating in the school seemed to be cranked in winter so that it was always overly warm. When the weather got nice outside, they all froze to death indoors. She would guess no one had informed the district they were having summer school because the air-conditioning seemed to be in some kind of low-power mode. Cat had been drinking ice water all morning, thinking of ways to cool off.

That and walking around was serving to keep her awake.

With Simon in one of her armchairs all night—after he'd fallen asleep in the middle of their conversation—she had been acutely aware she wasn't alone in her apartment. Not in a way that gave her any kind of unease, apart from the lingering effect of the story he had told her. She hadn't slept well, though.

He had survived a nightmare.

Stories like that weren't unheard of, and abuse happened more often than a lot of people wanted to believe. Being a cop and working in a school had given her insight into things most people didn't want to know.

Like how strong life required some people to be.

She hadn't stopped praying for Marianna, wherever the girl was. The police and Vanguard were looking for her. Cat and Simon were going to have a meeting with everyone later to discuss what Peter had said about this not being a single incident of abduction, but more than one missing person.

Cat watched Simon for a second longer and then moved on. Just as with him and the surveillance he was doing on Justice Spears, Cat couldn't let anyone realize she was far too attentive to the new teacher. Even if they believed it was because she was the School Resource Officer and wanted to make sure everyone was safe, she shouldn't draw attention to him.

Cat checked on the other classes, walking the hall between the front entrance and the cafeteria. She was almost at the double doors when her phone rang.

She didn't recognize the number. "Officer Alvarez."

A gruff voice replied, "Arlo told me you visited him."

Cat frowned, turning back to head toward her office. Who was this? They evidently knew the kid who'd confessed to shooting her. "What's it to you?"

This could either be a warning to leave him alone or

someone with information that might help her solve the case everyone else seemed to think was closed.

She passed an older man walking with Principal Cruise. As she walked by them, the older man winked at her. The visitor badge he had clipped to his shirt pocket would only be valid for today, but as this man was a Vanguard employee supposedly working on the IT network, he would be here for as many days as it took.

The company wasn't wasting any time making sure Simon had the support he needed, even if he didn't want it. And the person placed inside the school couldn't be Peter as it would be far too obvious to the students that they were twins.

The gruff voice said, "He's my cousin. That's what it is to me." He paused for a second. "You think he's innocent?"

Arlo hadn't seemed too interested in what she had to say. But for some reason, this cousin of his was? He had to have passed the information about her to this man. Maybe there was a person in Arlo's life smart enough to see that this wasn't what his fate was supposed to be. That he should never have thrown his life away by falsely testifying that he had killed a police officer and shot another.

"I was there." Cat gripped the phone. "The shooter killed my partner and shot me in the leg. But I never saw his face well enough to be able to identify him." It was why the prosecutor had relied more on the confession than on her statement or any other witness testimony.

"You think he lied?"

"It might not matter what I think." She closed the door to her office, rounded the metal desk, and sat, shaking the mouse to wake her computer up before she entered her login password.

"I want to talk. Face-to-face," he said. "If you think he's innocent, then we should meet."

Cat needed to get something straight. "I don't think he's innocent. I just think he might not have done this."

He rattled off a street address.

"I'll have to come by on my lunch break." She wouldn't miss the meeting after work with Vanguard and the police department.

The call ended.

Okay, then. She stared at her phone, then typed the address into her computer. A tire shop not too far from here, probably about ten minutes' drive. There was nothing about it that popped up on the police radar, which didn't necessarily mean it was clean.

Thirty minutes later, Cat pulled up just down the street from the garage. She sat for a moment and watched two men talk outside, then shake hands. One guy got into his car and drove off. The other stood by the open garage doors and looked around. He slid a pack from his pocket and lit a cigarette.

She left her jacket off so that her badge and gun would be clearly displayed. Anyone who saw her would know she was a cop. It could cause some problems for whoever this guy was if people saw him talking to a police officer, but this was about protecting herself first before she did a favor for someone else.

He spotted her approach and lifted his chin. "You her?"

"Alvarez."

He frowned. "I met another cop named Alvarez. A guy."

"Probably my brother, or if it was years ago, it might've been my father." Or one of her uncles, although that was a stretch.

"Younger guy."

But he wasn't going to tell her the context of that meeting? She would have to follow up with Romeo and find out what happened. "And you are?"

"Carlos." He took a drag from his cigarette and blew it off to the side. "Why are you bothering my cousin talking about how he lied or whatever? You think that's going to help him do what he's gotta do?"

Cat shrugged one shoulder. "You asked me here to tell me to leave him alone?"

He flicked the cigarette, dislodging ash from the end. "Seems like he'd be better served with you working out who did kill that cop instead of putting ideas in his head about getting out."

So it was more that he simply didn't want his cousin to get his hopes up. "If I'm going to solve the case, I need to know what he knows. Who asked him to lie? Does he know who the real killer is?"

Someone dangerous was still out on the street, and a young man had thrown his life away, going to jail for a crime he didn't commit. Given the way she was raised—by a cop who followed the Lord as if God was not just heavenly Father but also his commanding officer who issued orders and dictated the way a person should live—the sense of justice that lived deep inside her grated against Arlo's fate.

Her father thought logically about spiritual things. He saw the world in black and white, right and wrong. The same way her dad thought logically about the law, he thought about everything.

In her experience, evil often disguised itself as good. It was sometimes hard to tell what lay under the surface in this morally gray world. The place where people's true intentions lay, and who was truly innocent, was often buried deep.

"Arlo doesn't know anything." Carlos sucked on the cigarette and blew it out again. "Stop asking."

"He has to know who ordered it." She stared at him because she had few moves other than this. "Why don't you give me the person's name so I can start ruffling feathers on both sides?"

Carlos snorted. "Are you really sure you want to do that?"

"It's all wrong, and I want to make it right." Though, she'd received his warning. She wasn't going to put herself and people she cared about at risk without evidence.

"'Make it right.'" He scoffed. "That's a nice dreamworld you're living in, but it isn't this one. Things happen, and there ain't nothin' you can do about it." Carlos shot her a look. "But if you want to try and save Arlo's soul, then go right ahead. Don't blame me if it backfires."

She didn't move. "Who ordered Arlo to confess to murder?"

Carlos shook his head. Maybe for her benefit, or the benefit of someone he thought was watching. Given he was standing in plain view talking to a cop, he might want anyone observing him to think he wasn't telling the cop anything. "Guy's name is Hayden. Look him up."

"I can't harass him without probable cause."

He took a step back. "I can't help you. Leave Arlo alone." Carlos stuck his cigarette into the top of a pedestal trash can made of metal that seemed to have been placed there precisely for the purpose of disposing of butts.

Cat headed back to her car. She turned on the engine and immediately dialed her brother's number. It was early afternoon, so there was a chance he would be awake.

"Alvarez."

"Funny," she said. "That's how I answer the phone as well."

He let out a sigh, and she heard a sound a lot like when he'd flop on the couch. "Everything good?"

"I just chatted with Carlos over at the tire shop on

Manchester Road. He's the cousin of the kid who confessed to shooting me and Sergeant Ellis."

Romeo said nothing.

Waiting for her to explain why she had called?

"He knows Arlo didn't do it. He mentioned a guy named Hayden. You know anything about him?"

She pulled onto the street and turned the car around to head back toward the school. Minimal traffic, given this was a more residential area, but enough cars that she ended up in a line in the turn lane waiting for the light to go green.

"If it's who I think it is, he's bad news. A midlevel guy, but he's working his way to becoming untouchable."

"Who is he connected to?"

Romeo said, "The group is based in the neighborhood behind the school, to the north. One of the center houses. That's where you'll find him."

"Text me the address." She could do a drive-by later tonight, see what she could see.

"No, I'm not going to do that." Romeo's tone didn't invite any argument whatsoever. "I'll put a note in and request extra patrols tonight. Maybe have them canvas and ask about the missing girl. But it's not something you're going to do. Pretty sure that's outside of your scope of duties as the School Resource Officer."

Cat opened her mouth to object. Before she could, a car weaved around her in the right lane and cut her off before moving to the right lane again. "What on earth..."

"What is it?" Romeo sounded alert now.

"Just some idiot who doesn't know how to stay in his lane."

The window rolled down on the left side, behind the driver. Cat gripped the wheel, about to hit the brakes or make a turn. Just in case.

Something flew out of the window and hit the front of her car, square in the center of the hood. Paint sprayed up the hood and hit the windshield. Glass splintered.

She cried out and fought for control of the car, completely unable to see what was in front of her.

I'm going to crash!

FOURTEEN

A handful of the kids had chosen to eat their lunch in Simon's classroom. A couple of girls and Justice Spears, plus his buddies. Simon occupied himself with his laptop until Justice got up to toss his sub sandwich wrapper into the trash by Simon's desk. Something he shouldn't do, since it was only for paper. Technically, the kid needed to head all the way down to the cafeteria and dispose of the food wrapper in the big trash cans designated for that.

The teacher who used this classroom during the school year wasn't going to want ants.

For the sake of the case, Simon wouldn't mention it this first time it happened. He glanced over, leaned slightly toward the kid, and asked, "How did you do earlier on the quiz?"

There wasn't much about the kid that came across as childish. He was a high school junior and probably passed for someone in his early twenties. Simon would put money down on the fact this kid had a fake ID. He probably used it to buy whatever he wanted, along with his father's credit card.

Justice sniffed, shrugged. "I guess I did okay."

"Anything you want to go over? I'm thinking you'll pass the class at least, but I can fill in any gaps if you want."

Everyone knew that gaps in math learning could cause a lack of understanding later, at a higher level. Although maybe everyone didn't know that, and Simon simply assumed they did.

His experience of interacting with regular people was limited. What was normal supposed to be like? He had always stuck out to an extent. It was definitely easier to blend in as an adult. But even at Vanguard, he seemed to be an anomaly. To be fair, they hadn't ever given him the impression that was a bad thing.

The kid shrugged again.

"When something is hard, it makes a difference whether you believe you can do it or not." Simon tried to sound teacherly. "The mind is powerful, and we can block our own progress just because we don't think we can do something."

Peter's suggestion that they should begin with this one person and flip the teenager to roll over on his family wasn't a bad idea. But targeting a young man didn't sit right with him. Not when it was unclear which of Justice's family members were involved.

Justice might be in the middle of everything and as guilty as all of them. Or he might be trapped with no choice. The way the family had trapped Simon.

Justice said, "Football's the same way. Coach said if you don't believe you can catch the ball, then you'll drop it."

"Principles that apply to all kinds of things. Not just football." Of course, football was a mystery to Simon. He'd read a book one time that had explained the game and the rules and how it all worked, but the book didn't tell him why anyone would want to get all banged up like that.

Justice wandered back to his seat, where one of his friends spoke quietly to him. Justice shook his head.

Simon was entirely too focused on the case to worry about whether they liked him as a teacher. He could see the appeal of imparting learning into young minds and the rush of solving a case Peter got from success in a mission. Just like when Simon hacked a secure system and gained access.

But with his job, there were no lives at risk. When he messed with computers, no young minds would be forever altered by the things he said and did.

Even though this mission could fix what was broken inside him, it could, at the same time, cause harm to Justice. But what other choice was there? Justice was the gateway to his father or some other relative—maybe an uncle.

When Simon had run from the estate the night he escaped, he'd been chased by dogs and men with guns. It was only luck, or providence, that a delivery driver was on the street the moment he ran out into the middle of the road.

Maybe the driver knew exactly what happened on that estate because he'd said nothing about the crazed way Simon looked.

Simon had never been able to track the guy down. Or the road.

The bell rang, and the kids filed out. A minute or so later, an older man strolled in wearing jeans and a faded denim shirt with a visitor's badge clipped to his shirt pocket. Bob Davis ran the Cold Case department at Vanguard. Peter's boss, technically. They were close, and Simon occasionally got caught in that net, though not so much lately when Peter spent most of his time with Selena.

As much as he tried to get used to his life and the way it had been for a while, things were constantly changing.

Simon asked, "Are you going to tell me I'll lose my job if I don't let Vanguard help me?"

Bob set his phone on the desk. "I don't need you to let me help you. I'm already here."

"Under what pretense?"

Bob grinned. "I'm just the IT guy. Doing a spot check on the network."

"Funny, because I recall you needing help just to print a PDF." Simon snorted.

Bob chuckled. "Guess you should keep an eye on me, then you can make sure you fix whatever I break." The old man frowned slightly. "Did you get anything from the kid just a second ago?"

So he had seen Simon talking to Justice Spears. "Trying to establish a rapport, mostly."

Bob asked, "But you and your NSA friend got into the network?"

Simon nodded. "We're trying to figure out the center of the nexus."

"The person who forced you to create it."

Here it was. The information Peter wanted to gain from Simon but couldn't come here to ask himself. All the students would notice if Simon's twin suddenly showed up pretending to be unrelated to him. They were way too similar looking, even with different hairstyles.

"We need the location of the server."

"You need to tell us what the guy's name is. Or her." Bob shrugged, but there was nothing nonchalant about it. "We need to do a full work-up on the person that took you."

How on earth was he supposed to explain that?

Before he could figure out what to say, commotion erupted in the hallway. Voices filtered down to him. Snatches of broken conversation.

"...know that, Romeo. You don't have to keep saying it."

Simon pushed back his chair and strode to the doorway. He spotted Romeo in plain clothes walking beside Cat, who looked frazzled. He watched them approach, and when she spotted him, he shook his head, asking silently what was going on.

Cat's brother looked a little exasperated. "I need more than what you're giving me, or there's nothing I can do about what happened to you."

She hung back a step, then moved behind him and headed for Simon. "Hey. Everything okay here?"

"Yeah," Simon said. "What happened when you went out for lunch?"

Romeo stepped up beside them. "That's the thing. She didn't go out for lunch. She took a meeting with a guy in a shady tire shop."

"Just because a tire shop is in a run-down part of Benson doesn't mean it's shady." Cat put a hand on her hip. "There might be nothing illegitimate about it, and if you can't prove otherwise, then you're just being prejudiced."

Simon asked, "What happened?"

He'd seen her leave through the window and had almost texted her to ask if she could pick him up something.

Cat brushed hair back from her face that had come loose from her ponytail. "I got into an altercation with another car, and Romeo picked me up. All we need to do now is wash my car."

There was definitely more to it than that. Was her hesitation to share due to her brother's presence here or because she didn't want Simon to be concerned?

Romeo said, "Some guy tossed a paint can onto the front of her car. She could have been killed."

"I'm not downplaying the risk. I'm just saying that no harm came of it except my shattered windshield."

"Did it have anything to do with the meeting you went to?" Simon stuck his hands in his slacks pockets. The phone he had in his possession, the one that no one had the number to, was vibrating. "Did someone follow you, maybe?"

"I doubt Carlos sicced anyone on me. Doesn't seem like his style." Cat shifted her weight from one foot to the other. "I got the feeling he wants me to look into the person who coerced Arlo into confessing."

Bob shifted a lot closer to their huddle. "It might not be a cold case, but solving mysteries is what my department does. Especially when there are no obvious leads to explain what happened."

Romeo shook his head. "The police department doesn't need Vanguard's help on a case where a conviction has already been made. The shooter is in prison."

Cat glanced at her brother. "And the fact I don't believe he did it isn't relevant?"

"That's not what I'm saying." Romeo ran a hand through his hair. "You've been through enough. You don't need to be worrying about this."

Cat said, "I'm not trying to heal anymore. This isn't about what I went through. It's about getting a shooter off the streets."

Her words were strong and her face stoic. No lingering fear. Whatever had happened on the street might have shaken her initially, but she had worked through the reaction. Probably using skills she learned in the group she attended. The one Jasper was forcing him to be a part of for at least three more weeks.

His job was no longer a sure thing.

His new boss wanted to put that all in jeopardy.

Bob said, "Regardless of how the PD feels about me, Vanguard can help add resources so the police department isn't using theirs." The older man shrugged.

Simon spun to him. "If the police department has a problem with you, then they have a problem with the whole of Vanguard."

At the edge of his vision, Romeo shifted. He did have a problem with Bob—and Vanguard.

That wasn't good.

It also wasn't Simon's job to convince Romeo they were good people. The guy would either see the truth and believe it, or he would continue believing the worst with no evidence. Yet another prejudice? Romeo Alvarez seemed like an interesting guy with a whole lot of opinions that he might do better to keep to himself.

Bob shifted slightly. "We all know what we're up against."

Cat raised her hand. "I don't."

Simon said, "Bob made a mistake, and he did his time. Either the system works or it doesn't, and what are cops even doing arresting people and forcing them before a judge if there's a flaw in rehabilitating criminals?"

Bob looked at Cat and said, "It wasn't a violent crime. It was police corruption."

Cat said, "Ah. I wonder if you knew our father, Warren Alvarez."

Bob nodded. "We have lunch once a month now at the diner on Fifth Street. Your father is a good man."

Romeo spun around and wandered off, pulling out his phone.

Bob asked, "Are you sure you're all right?"

Cat nodded. "Thank you."

"Let me know if there's anything Vanguard can do for you." Bob walked away also.

Simon wanted to tug Cat against his side and give her a hug. Instead, he glanced at the clock. Only minutes before lunch was over. "Did the person you met with give you any intel?"

"Maybe the person that convinced Arlo to testify."

Simon's brows rose.

"He gave me the name Hayden."

FIFTEEN

Cat didn't need her brother wading into her life, despite the fact that he did it frequently. If he hadn't shown up so quickly after she'd pulled over, she would have called dispatch and asked for a black-and-white to her location.

Since she'd been on the phone with Romeo at the time that paint splashed across her windshield, there had been no point. Cat could easily file the report later. No one needed to miss another call that could be more important just to take down information from her.

Then again, given the way he reacted, maybe she should have called dispatch and told her brother not to come.

She shook her head. "I really can't believe Romeo sometimes. I'm sorry. He can get hotheaded."

Simon glanced up at her. "Huh?"

What had his thoughts so occupied? Between Bob, her brother, her lunch meeting, and what happened to her after, it could be any of those things that Simon was currently absorbed with. "What is it?"

Hopefully, it wasn't about her brother. Romeo wanted to

protect her, and the idea she was even close to regular police duties seemed to flip a switch in him. He believed in the police department. He lived by the sense of justice they'd been raised to put their faith in, almost as much as the Bible, and it ran blue when he bled for the department.

Like when he'd been blown up a couple of years ago. Some incident in a house involving the FBI here in Benson, one of whom was Bob's daughter. That had taken her a second to piece together. The connection between Bob, the FBI, the detective Lucas, and Vanguard.

Romeo probably liked that she was as much out of the loop as she found herself to be. But Cat would ask the questions so she wasn't blindsided by things she should be privy to.

Simon looked at his shoes again, then up at her. "You said Hayden?"

She nodded. "You know him?"

"I followed Justice when he left on the first day of school. I overheard him and the guy he called Hayden talking about getting ready for something. The guy was gonna 'take care of him.'"

Most likely that had to do with drugs. Just because the kids who attended the school were underage didn't mean they had no access to substances that could easily be abused. She hadn't even drank coffee when she was in high school.

Cat asked, "What do you mean you heard them talking?"

Simon winced. "Don't ask questions when the answer makes you an accessory to a possible crime. Probably best not to know."

Her eyebrows rose. "At least you didn't say an accessory to a Vanguard operation."

He conceded that with a nod. "So, the kid who confessed to shooting you and your partner is connected to the same guy?"

"He killed my partner. I only caught a bullet in the leg."

Simon shook his head for some reason. "He was trying to kill both of you. He just missed when it came to you."

Her eyes burned.

She glanced down the hallway at the board on the wall where art projects had been hung last semester and never taken down. Creativity, and a display of all the angst and hope. The pressure and dreams contained in teenage minds.

"You shouldn't downplay it. You didn't *only* get shot in the leg. It was murder and attempted murder, right?" He shifted closer to her and lowered his voice. "Those were the charges?"

Cat nodded.

He laid a hand on her shoulder and squeezed. "I guess we'd better figure out who this Hayden guy is and what he's connected to."

The note in his voice and the shadow in his expression gave her pause. Was there something he hadn't yet shared with her? Another trauma, or a piece of the puzzle that made up the complex image of his experience. Light and shadows, hard edges, and curves. No experience occurred cleanly. Not when people and pain were involved.

"Did your car really get hit with paint?"

She nodded again, grateful for the reprieve from heavier subjects. "It's all over my hood and my windshield, which is shattered. I used the wipers and got to the side of the road, but they had already driven off. I never even saw the license plate."

"It could have been caught on a street camera. I'll call Peter and see what he can find?"

Thankfully, he phrased it like a question. "For the record, I'm open to any and all assistance from Vanguard." She gave that a second to sink in. "Maybe it's the fact that I've been out of regular police work for so long that makes me not as territorial as other cops. They don't want help, and they will swear up and down they don't need it."

Simon gave her a small smile. "The Cold Case department frequently runs into roadblocks with the police. No one wants to admit they weren't able to solve a case."

She shrugged one shoulder. "Everyone needs a little help sometimes or fresh eyes on something."

If he agreed with her, would he also agree to let her in on every part of what he was doing? Maybe she wouldn't understand all the technobabble regarding his communication network. But she understood how to look at something with the eyes of an investigator, and that might be exactly what he needed.

She might be exactly what he needed.

Cat cleared her throat. "Maybe later, if we confirm they are the same person, we can share notes about what we're working on. Pool our resources and see if we can figure this out."

Simon's face relaxed, and he said, "That would be good."

His stomach rumbled.

He chuckled, and she was about to comment when an alarm chimed over the school announcement system, echoing loudly down the hall. "This is an emergency situation. All students and staff please proceed to the north field to assemble away from the building. Repeat, this is an emergency situation."

Doors opened, and kids filed out of classrooms, heading toward the end of the hall behind her where the double doors led outside.

"What does that announcement mean?"

She tugged him out of the way of students headed toward

the doors. A younger male student shoved another, and they nearly both slammed into a locker.

Cat called out to them, "Just head outside. No running or messing around, guys." She turned to Simon. "We don't say it, but that's the announcement that means there has been a bomb threat made against the school."

She motioned for him to walk with her, and she checked classrooms as she went. Cat would have to show him where to go outside, and then she needed to do another sweep of the building for students or staff members who might still be inside.

Simon pushed out the double doors where the crowd of students trailed off into the field and gathered in groups. Staff members waved their arms, and Principal Cruise shielded her eyes from the sun. "Quickly now. Everyone to your classes."

The students moved slowly, grouping themselves in the correct areas.

Cat said, "Head for your math kids."

Simon whirled around. "What are you going to do?"

"My job. So when you see the fire department or police officers show up, tell them I'm doing my sweep."

She heard the doors shut behind her, and thankfully, he didn't follow or argue. He still had to keep up the pretense of doing his job, even though that wasn't why he was here this summer. Cat headed for her office and lifted her radio from the charging dock. She grabbed the second one, assuming she would run into Romeo. He probably hadn't left yet. Did he have a radio with him?

She turned on the radio and held down the button on the side. "Alvarez Two-Eight, this is Alvarez Three-One. Come in."

Romeo stuck his head out of the main office, where the

door had been propped open. "I don't have anything. What's going on? The secretary said this is a bomb threat."

Lauren, the secretary, hurried out of the office and down the hall toward the doors.

Romeo looked almost sad to see the young woman go. Cat handed him a radio, resisting the urge to roll her eyes. "You take the west halls. Go classroom by classroom. Make sure no one is hanging back. We need everyone out of here."

Romeo glanced around. "What about closets and such?"

Cat said, "Open every door and check behind it."

"Copy that."

They split up and searched the whole building, meeting back at the office. Cat found two students reading books in a quiet corner of the band room and kicked them outside. The rest was clear, and Romeo reported the same thing back to her.

Two firefighters in full turnout gear shoved the doors open and strode in, followed by a third. The one in front had tanned skin and a wide smile. "Romes."

Cat would never get over all the different versions of a name men came up with.

"Captain Julio Espinoza-Vasquez, this is Catalina Alvarez. My sister." Her brother added that last part as if it was an important piece of information.

"Officer Alvarez." She stuck out her hand, and Julio shook with her. "Though, I can see how that would get confusing with the two of us. So you can call me Cat."

The fire captain grinned. "I'm not confused in the slightest."

Romeo asked, "Should we go outside if there's a bomb threat?"

Cat told the fire captain, "We swept the building, and

there are no more people inside. I didn't see any sign of an explosive device anywhere. You?" She glanced at Romeo.

Her brother shook his head.

Captain Espinoza-Vasquez pointed to the door. "Outside is correct. Thank you."

Since they were being duly dismissed, Cat headed to the door first. Outside, a couple of police cruisers pulled up to the curb. Officers climbed out of one. Two detectives got out of the other, guys she recognized from seeing them in passing. They all strode over.

The bomb squad in Benson was comprised of personnel from different departments. Police, fire, and emergency services. That way, they had people trained in multiple disciplines, including emergency medical response.

Romeo tapped the outside of her arm. Principal Cruise headed down the side of the main building with a clipboard in her hand.

She spotted Cat and raised the clipboard, waving it. "We are still missing one student. Consensus with the ones we have gathered out back is that she likely went home when she heard the announcement. They think she figured nothing would be happening for the rest of the day."

"Maybe." Cat frowned. "But they all know they're supposed to check in even if they're going to leave."

Romeo said, "I'll tell Espinoza-Vasquez." He turned and jogged back to the building, already on his radio.

The way he moved was almost like he was unafraid. But then, he'd been caught in a bomb explosion before. The house where he had responded on a police call had blown up, tossing Romeo into the air. For a few days, he had been in critical condition, fighting for his life. The swelling on his brain had gone down quickly, and he had recovered almost as rapidly as the incident itself had happened.

Cat and her mom had prayed through every minute of it.

Two weeks later, Cat had applied for the police department, wanting to make a difference in a real way, just as Romeo did every time he put the uniform on. No one in her life thought it was a good idea for her to be a police officer. They'd all supported her becoming a School Resource Officer.

She tried not to think about what that meant for her. Or how much faith they had in her abilities.

The officers who'd shown up got the lowdown from the principal. All of them could deal with the situation here.

Cat said, "She may have gone home. If she isn't here, then I'll head to her house and find out if she's safe there."

And she was going to ask Simon if he wanted to go with her.

SIXTEEN

Simon glanced at the server. "Thanks." He picked up his fork and stabbed a piece of sausage in his pasta dish. "I always get this when I come here. It's really good."

Across from him at the table in Backdraft bar and grill, Cat smiled around a bite of her burger. "One of these days, I'm going to buy myself a gas grill for my balcony and learn how to use it so I can make these at home instead of spending fifteen dollars on one." After she had enjoyed the bite, she said, "But they do it so well."

He smiled back at her.

After the bomb squad had wrapped up a search of the building and found no explosive device, the school day had been practically over. No parents wanted their kids in the school after a scare like that, so everyone had been sent home.

He and Cat had gone to the missing girl's house, but she hadn't been there. Her mom wasn't worried, although she had sounded busy at work. The woman had promised to call if the girl didn't return home or if she couldn't get in contact with her at all by the end of the day.

The idea that this might be more than one missing person soured Simon's stomach like the time he had accidentally drank out-of-date milk. Peter had suffered more than him with the milk, actually throwing up, but Simon's nausea had been bad enough. It might have been better to simply throw up the spoiled drink. That wasn't how it had gone down, though.

He shook some salt and pepper on his meal and took a drink of soda.

Spending time with Cat like this made him wish the case was done and they could relax together. Then again, being friends and in each other's company was only going to make him wonder if there could be more between them.

She knew more about him than any of the women he'd dated in the last few years. He tried to keep things separate, but with Cat, it was as though worlds were colliding. Walls were coming down between things he normally didn't allow to mix. His history. The present. Work and his life outside work, which didn't usually amount to much when he wasn't seeing anyone.

She seemed comfortable in a place like this. He'd never brought his ex here because she always insisted on going somewhere "nice." Which meant expensive. Hopefully, Peter would show up late so Simon could spend more time alone with Cat.

She eyed him, squinting slightly. "What are you thinking about?"

"I doubt you want to know." Certainly not the details about the less than half dozen people he had been in a relationship with since high school.

"Try me."

Simon shook his head, smiling. Peter was more the kind to rise to a challenge, but this time, there wasn't much to lose when she already knew so much about him.

He set his fork down. "She doesn't work there anymore, but Lena was Clare's assistant at Vanguard. Now Clare doesn't really work there much of the time. Jasper, who used to be a police detective, is the new operations manager. Since Clare had her baby, she doesn't do much but oversee things at Vanguard from a distance. Anyway, Lena was Clare's assistant."

"I feel like you are revving your engine, gearing up to something. Is it really that terrible?"

Simon winced. And not because he had done anything. "Lena was the last person I went out with. And it was almost a year ago, I think. Maybe longer than that."

"What happened?" Her expression softened in a way he would've liked to have seen when he had been telling her that story in the dark. But at the same time, it was better to tell her without worrying about her reaction or if she'd realize how difficult it had been to say all that out loud.

Simon eased back in his chair. "It was a few weeks, and I was kind of swept up in it. Maybe too much. She was dating Peter at the same time, and neither of us were supposed to talk about the relationship, so we didn't figure it out until the damage was done."

They had unpacked it some, but not much. Maybe there were too many things they had never talked about. Things where they had a kind of silent understanding when they probably shouldn't.

Did that need to change?

Cat gasped. "She was two-timing you both?"

Simon nodded. "She got fired not long after. Clare didn't want someone with low morals working for her. She needs people on her payroll that have integrity and don't lie about huge things."

Cat said, "Seriously. That's crazy."

He took another bite, trying to figure out what else he should tell her. If she didn't write him off after what he'd been through and that he hadn't been able to fight off the initial abduction, then the fact he'd killed a man in order to save his own skin...

She would probably call it quits with this friendship, plus a whole lot of attraction, now that she knew he was even more of a loser than she thought.

She pulled out her phone, not saying anything while she tapped and swiped through to a screen that she turned to show him.

A stupidly good-looking guy with a model-attractive woman and a tiny baby, all smiling at the camera.

He swallowed the bite he'd been working on and sipped his soda. "Who are they?"

Cat made a face. "That is my ex-boyfriend. Ex fiancé. Ex —whatever we were, because we exchanged promise rings, and we were making plans for the future."

Simon stared at her.

"He's the youth pastor at the church I used to go to, and that is his wife and their new baby. One minute, he's making promises to me, and then suddenly, we're over. Three weeks later, he's married to her, and seven months after that, she has their baby."

He had been two-timing her the way Lena did with Simon? He winced. "Ouch."

"Yeah." Cat shot him a sardonic look. "When I confronted him, he straight up told me I wasn't the kind of woman built to be a pastor's wife."

Simon couldn't believe it.

"I'm not sure if it's the fact I'm not blonde or that I'm not stick thin. Or the fact I wouldn't..."

"Uh-huh." No need to talk about boundaries and how

they seemed to have been nonexistent with Lena. Thankfully, he'd been smart about it, but it wasn't his finest moment. Especially knowing now she'd also been trying to have the same kind of relationship with Peter.

His brother had been more upstanding their whole lives, so it wasn't entirely a surprise.

He said, "We've all done things we aren't proud of. It probably feels pretty good you stuck to your guns on that one."

How could he find the balance between living under a silent cloud of shame and telling the whole world about his fears and failures? Not talking about things that happened to him or things that he'd done probably wasn't helping him to be free of the past. He could only do his best in the present. No expectations, no obligations. No one else got to tell him what to do, because everything he had learned about the world and the people who lived in it had taught him not to give up control over his choices.

She studied him for a second. What was she thinking? It might be better not to know. She obviously had faith and probably had something to say about the way he'd lived his life. As far as he could tell, it wasn't about good or bad and which a person claimed they were. It was more about what you had to show for it—like the fruit of good works the Bible talked about.

Her attention shifted to the side, and he turned just in time to see his brother slide in on the bench seat next to him. "Hey."

Peter leaned over and grabbed his fork, stealing a bite of Simon's dinner. "Hey." He shoved the huge forkful of pasta into his mouth, swallowing before he asked, "Ready for an update?"

This wasn't exactly an update, more like a sharing of

information. But if he asked for that, then Peter—and the rest of Vanguard—might want him to share everything he knew. Maybe he could tell Peter and have his brother relay the information. No one would let him get away with that, though.

Peter glanced over and gave him a look.

Simon said, "Tell us the update."

His brother dug a flash drive out of his pocket and handed it to Cat. "Three other missing girls. So that gives us five total in the last two weeks. Plus, something else we're trying to track down, but the information for that isn't on the drive. What's there is everything we've dug up about the missing girls. Each one is between fifteen and nineteen."

"And they all appear to have been abducted by the same person?" Cat tucked the flash drive into her pocket.

"There is barely anything as far as intel on where they were taken or how, so we have no idea. We also don't have any witnesses who might have seen the abductor." Peter took another bite of Simon's dinner and dragged over the little electronic tablet, where he scrolled through the menu to order a meal of his own.

Simon used the distraction to retrieve his fork and slide the huge bowl of pasta back in front of him. Peter grabbed his drink and helped himself.

"So, these may not even be abductions," Cat said, a slight smile curling her lips. "Could be they ran away, maybe even in a pact, where they planned to meet up somewhere. Friends who stick together and they all want to start a new life somewhere else."

Peter said, "Possible."

Simon glanced at his twin. "But you think it's unlikely?"

"Only because of the other thing we're working on." Peter glanced at Cat. "When I have something concrete on that, I will let you know."

Based on her raised brows, she wasn't convinced. Probably due to the police department friction with Vanguard, who certainly chose to follow their own procedures and rules. That was why people went to work for them rather than the police department. But there was a whole lot of respect on both sides. Just not favors or looking the other way.

Which was exactly how it should be.

"Thanks." Cat took another bite of her dinner. Her attention snagged on something behind them, the way it had when Peter came in.

A woman with long dark hair, wearing wide-leg jeans and a cropped shirt so that they could all see she had a belly button ring, stopped beside their table. "Are you Cat?" She didn't even look at Peter and Simon.

Cat wiped her mouth with her napkin. "What can I help you with?"

"Carlos told me to come talk to you."

Cat glanced at Simon, then slid out of her seat. "Let's find somewhere quiet."

He was about to tell her not to leave the dining room of the restaurant where he'd be able to keep an eye on them when she waved the woman to a nearby table.

"What's that about?"

Simon shrugged. "Carlos is the guy she talked to about the kid in jail."

"Something else I need to be working on aside from these disappearances?"

"I don't think she needs your help. And I would rather you focus on the girls that might be terrified right now."

Peter leaned over and nudged his shoulder.

"It's called empathy. It doesn't need to be a big deal."

Peter said, "I sent you a calendar invite to go get fitted for tuxes. Before you ask, you can wear canvas shoes as long as they are black. I'm pretty sure Selena is going to wear flip-flops under her dress."

Simon took another bite so he could give himself a minute. Cat and the young woman were in intense conversation.

"Can't avoid this. It's happening."

"I'm not avoiding anything." He'd lived with the fear for far too long. He needed to figure out how to get rid of it. But was that even possible? "I'll be there."

How could he let go of the terror?

SEVENTEEN

"Carlos called me after you talked to him." The woman across the table from her had introduced herself as Alayna, and at first, it had seemed she was older. But perhaps this woman was only a year or two younger than her. Putting her in her early twenties.

"What did he ask you to tell me?"

Alayna shifted her purse on her lap, then lifted a fork with one hand, turning it over so that it clinked on the tabletop.

Cat spotted some of the familiar signs of someone who had experienced trauma. There were plenty of things a person might be reluctant to speak about, but a painful experience had some typical tells. Many of the people at the group she went to had them. Probably, they noticed some in her as well.

"It's a show of good faith. That his intel about the...person he mentioned? That it's legit."

Cat nodded.

Carlos wanted to prove to her that what he'd said was accurate, and yet right after she left the tire shop, she'd had that incident with the paint can. The two had to be connected. Either Carlos was trying to misdirect her into believing he was behind it, or someone else had been watching her and had seen her go talk to him.

Alayna stared at the fork as she rotated it. "Something happened to me...two years ago."

Cat waited and allowed her to figure out where to start talking. Probing questions might be a good idea in police interrogations, but they weren't always the right tactic in talking with a survivor.

"I was walking home from work. It was a Thursday, after eleven. My car broke down, and my dad had it up on blocks, so I didn't have a way to get to and from work aside from walking." Alayna swallowed. The fork clattered to the tabletop. "Someone grabbed me. I think there were two of them, and they shoved me into a trunk. Tied me up and injected me with something. I remember feeling a needle."

The young woman sucked in a choppy breath.

Cat could guess what was coming, and it was likely similar to what Simon had been through. Either way, she'd survived. She had returned to her life, and the days had moved on. But Cat, of all people, understood that intense pain left a mark on a person that was not easily forgotten.

"I knew what was happening, but I couldn't do anything about it." Alayna sniffed. "They called it a party. I was in a hotel room, and I couldn't even stand up, let alone figure out how to get out of there." She cleared her throat. "Men came in and out. I couldn't do anything."

"But you escaped." How else would she have managed to get free?

"Three days, maybe four days later. Someone found me in an alley. An ambulance took me to the hospital, and the doctor said I'd overdosed."

If she had seen a doctor, there could very well be evidence. "Did they do a sexual assault exam?"

"The nurse was crying. She told me I would probably take weeks to heal, but that there was nothing found on me...as if someone had cleaned me. I have no idea how."

Cat bit her lip. "I'm sorry for what you went through."

She couldn't even imagine having to live with those kinds of questions. What she had survived was bad enough, but for Alayna to know things had happened that were out of her control. Nightmarish things that were buried somewhere in her mind. Maybe it was better that she didn't remember. It was possible that being drugged was a kind of mercy.

Sure, she hadn't been able to fight back or stop it. Alayna also had enough gaps in her memory that it was mostly only the blank of unanswered questions she had to live with. Not every second of it indelibly etched into her psyche.

Which would be worse? The memories, or the unanswered questions. "I go to this group. It's for survivors of any trauma. I can give you the information if you want."

Alayna said, "I don't need help."

"You know where to find me if you ever do. For anything." The tools for healing weren't a one-size-fits-all thing. Everyone dealt with their history in their own way, and not everyone wanted to talk it out in a group. "Thank you for sharing that with me. I can only imagine how hard it was to talk about it aloud."

Alayna shrugged a slender shoulder but said nothing.

Cat asked, "Do you know if it was just you or if there were more girls who were taken the same way?" After all, Vanguard seemed to believe more than one young girl had been abducted recently. Perhaps it was happening again.

Two years later. Long enough that no one would tie the incidents together.

"I don't know how many of us there were or who the others are. I just know they shoved me out of the car just like they grabbed me. And everyone pretended like it never happened."

Cat nodded. "All right. Thank you."

Alayna shifted in her seat. Maybe she had already said everything she came here to say.

Cat leaned forward in her chair. "Do you know if there's any connection between what happened to you and this Hayden person?"

Alayna flinched. "I try to stay as far away from anything to do with him as possible. I don't know what it is or if my mind can remember something, but he seriously gives me the creeps. He tried to steal Carlos's business from him. They were harassing him and pressuring him to sell the tire shop to them. He refused."

So there was something in it for him if the police had Hayden on their radar. Not just a show of good faith on Carlos's part, confirming that what he had told her was legit. But he was also handing her a possible witness—or at least good intel—that the police needed laser focus on Hayden. And in the end, Carlos would have one less headache.

Whether this Hayden person was connected to the more recent disappearances was something the police were going to have to prove. With strong enough evidence that there could be no doubt when it came down to the court case.

"Thank you for coming. Like I said, if you need anything—"

Alayna said, "Carlos takes care of me." She slid the chair back and nearly silently walked through the restaurant and out the door.

Cat closed her eyes for a second, giving her heart and mind a moment to process the enormity of what that girl had been through. She prayed for her and for any of the other victims who had been abducted around the same time. Then she prayed for Marianna and any other girl who had been taken now.

We need to find them.

Her need for justice, and the other innate traits that had been imprinted on who she was, refused to rest. Young women she knew might be in danger. It was one thing to understand abstractly that things like this happened in the world. But in her own community, right on her doorstep? That was another thing entirely.

A soft touch on her forearm caused her to open her eyes. Simon crouched beside her. She gave him a small smile, simply for noticing enough to come over. It meant that he cared. "I need to look at what's on this flash drive. Then I need to go to the meeting."

Vanguard and the police department were touching base later, but this just might be the kind of thing the FBI in Benson wanted to get involved with. They might even end up banding around words like "taskforce" and pooling a whole lot of resources to save these girls. If the same thing was happening all over again, that meant new leads and a fresh chance to stop whoever was behind this.

Simon asked, "Do you want to finish eating first?"

The remainder of her meal held no appeal, but it was probably a good idea to fortify herself for what lay ahead of them.

Peter and Simon settled back onto the seat across from her. She studied the similarities and differences between them, allowing her mind a reprieve. Even if the peace only lasted a moment. Then she explained everything Alayna had told her and this possible connection to what was happening now.

The twins shared a look. They seemed to communicate in a kind of shorthand that probably came from being in each other's lives so closely, enduring what they'd been through together.

Simon had told her some things about his childhood as a missionary kid and how it certainly hadn't been what anyone would expect that kind of life to be. Not just when his father turned out to be a criminal.

Then there was his past relationship, something that gave her serious pause. He lived what he believed. It was just that his convictions weren't like hers. Not that they were anything close to Pastor Tyler Cunningham and his betrayal. More like what she would assume from someone who wasn't a believer.

Cat had always trusted that God had prepared someone for her. But was that person really out there? Relationships seemed like so much of a gamble sometimes.

She might need to draw a boundary line between her and Simon that kept them firmly in their friend zone. At least until she knew for sure whether they were on the same page about certain things.

Peter said, "Vanguard can be a serious help to the police department."

She caught an expression on his face that she'd seen on Simon's and made an assumption as to what it meant. "You want me to persuade them to let you guys be all-in on this?"

The twins waited.

"I'm not prepared to risk a bunch of young women suffering the way Alayna did just to satisfy the police department's ego."

Peter nodded. "Vanguard isn't going to push and force them to allow Bob Davis back in the fold. But we can be a serious asset."

"Jasper is in charge now, and he used to be a cop." Cat

shrugged. "Surely, he's the one that can get everyone working together."

Simon glanced at his brother.

Peter said, "He can talk. But the action is going to come down to us and guys like Romeo."

Cat frowned. "And you don't have as much respect for Jasper now because he gave up his detective shield in order to be a manager in a suit taking meetings and making deals?"

Simon's brows rose, and he glanced at his brother. "Do you think that?"

"I respect the guy just fine." Peter shook his head. "I just prefer to be kicking doors down rather than wearing a tie. I don't know why anyone would give that up."

Cat said, "The money is probably better." Not just private sector, but more of a managerial position than working as an everyday detective with a schedule of rough hours and pulling overtime.

Simon tipped his head to the side. "Plus, he'll be married soon, and Destiny is pregnant. Life changes. People want different things—like a balance between their personal life and their work life."

"Or so you've heard?" Peter glanced at him.

The two of them shared an amused look.

There would always be something between the twins she couldn't be a part of. Cat wouldn't upset their balance by attempting to insert herself into something she had no place in. What they had was a bond no one else could touch. It was a beautiful thing to see, even if it made her a little envious that there was no one in her life she was that close to.

She finished her meal, and Peter got his to go. Romeo was having her car windshield fixed, then the car would be cleaned and detailed, so they had driven here in a vehicle Simon...

"Hang on a second." Halfway to the car, Cat spotted Simon's motorcycle in a space not far from it. She turned back to the twins and asked Simon, "Whose car is this?"

Peter said, "It's mine. So no funky smells, thanks."

He strode away, toward Simon's motorcycle. The twins had switched vehicles this afternoon. Because of the bomb threat, or because her car had been out of commission? "I feel like I missed an entire thing."

Simon put his hand on her back. "Come on, I'll explain on the way."

EIGHTEEN

Simon took a look at the conference room, fourth floor of the police department. He'd been here in this building exactly once, on the day he was walked in wearing handcuffs. Since then, he'd opted to steer clear of the place.

Cat stopped two paces in and turned back. "Come on, I always sit up front."

He wasn't an "up front" kind of guy.

She eyed him. "Or we can find somewhere in a corner where no one will notice you?"

"I'm not that bad."

Peter nudged his shoulder. "Yes, you are. It was weird for me the first time, too." His phone started to ring, so he tugged it out and stepped back into the hall. Probably Selena.

Simon's safety net was frequently drawn aside by the relationship that had given Peter something he'd always wanted. Simon didn't always get to lean on his brother and their connection. Often, he had to stand on his own, especially with his brother on more missions, or "operations," these days.

Cat studied him. "You okay?"

He nodded. "Show me where we're sitting."

She stuck close by him in the ocean of cops in uniform, plenty more in business clothes, and the FBI contingent from downstairs. Pretty much everyone had a white paper cup of coffee. Light streamed in the window, the bright yellow beam radiating heat across the middle rows until someone adjusted the blinds.

When she had settled into a chair that was a good compromise between the front row and hiding in the corner, he turned to her. He should probably explain. "Peter got a girlfriend last summer."

She glanced over at him.

"She's great. I'm not saying she isn't." He winced. "Actually, she's great for *him*. I'm happy for him. He's content in a way that he's never felt before."

"You can tell all that?"

"Sometimes, we get strong emotions that are each other's, not ours. When I'm with him...I feel better. When he's gone, I mostly focus on work, but occasionally, I get a rush of anxiety or fear, so I know something went down. But he texts me right after it's done. If he didn't, I'd call the Famous Ones, and they'd drag his butt out of wherever."

"Who?"

He said, "They're a Vanguard team. Retrieval, mostly. Getting people out of jams."

"They sound like good people to know."

He nodded, still thinking about the shared emotion part of being twins. Peter had never asked him about what happened when he was taken at seventeen. Who knew what had gone on at home during the days Simon was missing. Maybe something Peter didn't want to talk about, making it an agreed upon silence.

"He's getting married in a couple of months."

She squeezed his knee. "Need a date?"

As soon as she said it, she sort of blanched. Because she hadn't meant to say that aloud? He didn't mind that she had made that suggestion. If he was going to go with anyone...

"Yes, I actually do need a date." Simon forced himself not to hesitate. "Want to go with me?"

"I would." She gave him a nervous smile. "I'm all about friends supporting friends."

And here he'd been hopeful that she'd listened to two of his stories so far and hadn't run as far as she could as fast as she could. She'd heard the tragic tale of his abduction and his epic disaster of a relationship—the one he'd kidded himself was actually something good that might last.

On the heels of that, Peter had met Selena.

Simon had been pretty much wallowing since then, because of both things.

Now that he'd met Cat, his thoughts had traveled down the relationship road, even speculating if she might be "the one" he had been looking for but was unwilling to admit to himself he wanted.

And she'd just friend-zoned him?

His heart squeezed in his chest so hard he might be having some kind of attack. Apparently, listening to his stories only meant she understood what he'd been through. It didn't alter her opinion of him as a guy she could care for. Fall for. It just meant she was a quality person who could be a great friend.

And what if that wasn't what he wanted?

Peter sat down next to him.

Simon shook his head. His brother might've felt the reaction he just had, but there was no need to talk about it. Another unspoken agreement to not dissect every tiny thing.

"Did something just happen?" It sounded so innocent when she asked it like that.

He had to play it off. "Maybe. I'm sure Peter will tell us."

Peter gave him an odd look that Simon ignored. Before his brother could ask him questions, the police commissioner, Russ Franklin, stepped up to the podium in front.

"Okay, everyone. We'll keep this brief because I know you're all eager to get to work." The older man was a former Marshal and was the epitome of the word "grizzled" with his gray hair and gray beard. Hard stubbled cheeks and dark gray eyes. His arms and trunk were thick, and he pressed it all into a five-ten frame that probably hit like a linebacker.

Peter nudged him. Simon waved it off. Cat looked at him.

He let out a long sigh no one heard. The last thing he needed was the two of them digging it out of him. There had been enough confessions recently, and he was ready to get to work instead. Forget the friend thing and fix some things that had been broken for far too long. In him. In Benson.

Didn't matter.

After that, he could eat a whole pizza by himself and wallow in the fact he was falling for Catalina Alvarez. It was happening despite all the reasons he was a bad choice for her. And she'd just relegated him to "friend." Maybe *because* she realized he was a bad choice.

"We have a known suspect and at least four missing girls." Russ paused, and the silence had a weight to it that hung in the air. "Possibly more."

Simon's stomach flipped. Could he help find these girls? He'd been taught he didn't measure up. Who would with a twin like Peter? He had found his own thing since those awkward teenage years and had done a lot of work on having self-respect in his own right. Without Clare having to send him to a group or give him an ultimatum.

Still, the old insecurities he'd always carried came back to the forefront whether he liked it or not.

Maybe he would never measure up.

Peter nudged him again, not actually saying *pay attention,* but that's what he meant.

Russ said, "The next step is to find any additional connected suspects and find out if there are any more missing girls. Let's see if we can get any intel on who might be targeted."

All kinds of ideas popped into his mind.

The police could set up a sting operation if they knew the identity of the next teenage girl target, and they could snap the trap shut and capture suspects. Flip them for the boss's identity. Risky, but it could yield a result.

If Justice Spears was involved—which seemed likely given the conversation with him and the Hayden person at the garage—this might be the time to move on him. Follow him and see if he would lead them to the suspect. Or pull him in for questioning and find out what he knows.

Dig more into the phone network. Find out if there was chatter about a party.

Russ asked, "Questions?"

Someone asked what the PD was going to tell the general public and if there was a scheduled press conference.

Russ shook his head. "When we know what this is and have it tied up neatly, we'll make an announcement. Until then, anyone caught passing information to the media or public in any form will be written up." He barely paused for a breath. "I'll coordinate with Jasper Hollingsworth at Vanguard."

Someone cheered, dragging out the name Jasper as if congratulating the man when he wasn't even here.

Russ smiled. "Tasks will be delegated according to the

best use of resources. I want updates every four hours, starting at the top of the hour. So, get to work and find me something, or I'll have to ask what I pay you for."

Peter chuckled under his breath.

As far as motivation went, that had been a pretty good tactic. Some people might not be motivated by it, but the competitive officers in the room would jump at the chance to be the best. The high achievers wouldn't want to let down a man they respected who also happened to sign off on their paychecks.

In the end, cases would be solved.

Russ moved to the corner by the windows where several officers crowded around, asking him questions. Half the room got up, walked out, and, hopefully, got to work.

Peter twisted in his chair. "Where are you and Talia at on the communication network?"

Simon saw the unspoken question in his expression. This wasn't all his brother wanted to ask. He dug in his backpack and pulled out his laptop, booting it out of sleep mode. "We are in, and that means we can see everything that happens on it in real time: calls made, duration of calls, and texts sent and received. She's got a good chunk of information on the scope as a whole, but it won't give us the location of any of the phones or tell us who is using them."

Or the location of where it was all being hosted.

"How many phones in total?" Cat shifted to lean close to his arm.

He caught a hint of vanilla on her skin and swallowed hard. "Thirty-six."

Peter blew out a breath. "All connected to the guy who abducted you to create it? What about him?"

Simon tapped the screen of his laptop, and a live file Talia was working on opened. "This is a nexus of who knows who based on phone calls between two numbers and texts sent in one-to-one messages or group threads. From that information, we can put together some connections. Who is close, and who might only be acquaintances. Or who gives the orders, and what the hierarchy might look like."

A couple of cops, maybe three or four, turned to listen to them.

Peter asked, "Anything about a party in the conversation?"

"I'll work on that tonight." Hopefully, back at the Vanguard office without people staring at him.

"Aren't you the guy who—"

Peter's head whipped around. "Don't finish that." Then to Simon, he said, "Let's go. We need to get to work, not sit around here talking."

Simon stood, holding his laptop open, and slung his backpack on his shoulder. Cat broke off a conversation with the cop down the row to their right, an older guy she apparently knew, and came with them.

Out in the hall, Peter said, "I need what you have on the guy who took you."

Simon walked with him toward the elevator. Cat stayed behind them, so they didn't block the entire width of the hall, which was lined with officers. Some of them gave him disapproving looks. Or her, probably for associating with him. If only he could stop and yell, "I'm not hiding anything!" at the top of his voice.

"Sie."

He pushed out a breath. "I'll pass on all the profiles I've done on the family."

Peter frowned. "You don't know who took you?"

"I never saw his face." Simon leaned against the wall beside the elevator and focused only on Peter and Cat. As if backing up to a solid surface meant he was more safeguarded than being exposed. In a police station? He needed to get his head on straight.

Peter moved to stand close. The way Simon wanted Cat to. "But you know where you were?"

"The family estate. Don't ask me where. They must have dumped it. Or it's so far below the radar I have no chance of finding it." Simon gritted his teeth. "It could be anyone. The father, the son, the uncle. A cousin. I have no idea."

But he'd been trying to figure it out for years.

Peter nodded. "Give it to me." He thumped a hand on his chest. "I do this."

Simon stared at his brother. "Okay."

The elevator doors slid open. Peter nudged him in first. Simon dragged his feet, even if it was for the best that Peter did what he was good at. He would likely also get the rest of the Cold Case department at Vanguard to help. Or the whole company, whoever wasn't working on the missing girls.

But would they really be able to work out what he hadn't found an answer to in years? If only he could believe it. Life had taught him otherwise over and over again. *Don't trust because it will all fall apart. Don't hope because it won't happen.*

Before the elevator doors closed, a hand slammed against the left side. "Alvarez! We got a call, officer in distress!" A patrol sergeant came into view. "It's Romeo."

NINETEEN

Peter drove faster than she would have. Simon sat beside her in the back seat, his laptop still open. But he wasn't looking at it. He was looking at her.

The concern in his expression warmed her heart. She leaned over and put her head on his shoulder. Simon slid his hand over, and she didn't think about it. She just slid hers underneath and curled her fingers between his.

"A couple of years ago, Romeo was on shift, working. A house exploded. It had to do with this local group at a compound, the FBI agent who is Bob's daughter, and Detective Hummet. It was a whole thing, but the gist is that Romeo was in critical condition for a few days. He bounced back, but..."

She had to stop and collect herself.

"No one else was hurt?" Peter asked the question from the driver's seat but didn't turn his head.

"Other cops were there. I think Samantha Jesse got hurt." She bit her lip. "I was working at the movie theater. I'd just finished college and had no idea what I was going to do next. But when the call went out, I wasn't in the loop because I'm not a cop. They called my dad, who left me a voicemail. I couldn't check my phone until the end of my shift, which was two in the morning."

She sucked in a choppy breath. "I didn't know. I rushed over to the hospital, and it was full of cops who'd been there for hours."

Being left out of the loop had hurt so bad, knowing her brother had been fighting for his life and she might've missed the chance to say goodbye. She had seen only one way to be *in* the loop next time. Even though there would, hopefully, never be a repeat of that tormenting type of waiting. Praying. Hoping he would pull through.

"But he healed." Simon's breath brushed her forehead.

If she nodded, that would dislodge this closeness, so she stayed still. She'd used the f-word. *Friends.* Could she handle that? It would be far too hard to continue to get to know him, to learn even more amazing things about him and how strong he had to be to have survived, and watch him eventually fall for someone else.

Resigning them to being only friends was the safe option.

It left her without the need to take any steps. Or risk anything. Friendships had far more boundaries than a relationship. Of course, she took plenty of risks outside of relationships. She was the one who'd joined the police department when everyone said she didn't need to do that. Shouldn't. Couldn't. *Don't be silly.*

As if just being a girl, or being Catalina, meant she would get herself killed.

That wasn't what happened. It was her partner who had lost his life. Even if everyone knew she couldn't have stopped it, and it wasn't like Ellis had shoved her out of the way and taken the bullet, she still saw how the other officers looked at her. The whispers. The insinuation that she should have saved him.

Peter pulled over to the side of the street and parked, whipping into a tiny space that made her breath hitch. He shoved out his door a second later.

"Come on." Simon squeezed her hand and let go.

She hesitated. Why couldn't she just cling to him? Because she was a strong woman who stood on her own two feet. But couldn't she be both of those women?

Independent and reliant.

Brave and concerned.

A friend...and something more.

She slid over and got out on his side. Simon touched the small of her back and left his hand there. She asked, "Is it just me, or has this been the longest day ever?"

He smiled. "I slept in a chair last night."

Cat sighed. "I need some chair time." She glanced up at the sky. "Can't even see the stars downtown. There is way too much light."

He gave her an odd look but said nothing as they approached the crowd of cops. Onlookers. Emergency vehicles, mostly police cars and one ambulance. The rear doors were open, but since it was parked facing them, she couldn't see inside.

The officer on crowd control recognized her and lifted his chin. "Back of the bus."

"Thanks." She headed for the ambulance and peered around the doors the first chance she could get. "Romeo."

He sat on the gurney, his feet on the floor. Full uniform, all the stuff on his belt nudging the sheet under him. Slightly pink cheeks beneath his tanned skin. The EMT sat in front of him, shining a light at his face. He winced and turned to her, blood running down the side of his face.

Oh, no.

"Hey." She pressed her lips together.

"I'm fine."

Sure, except for the fact he slurred his words. Did he have a concussion? "You should go to the hospital."

He turned away from her and paled slightly but said nothing. That was about as much argument as he had the strength to muster up right now. Which was a serious problem. Her brother was supposed to be strong. Tough enough to withstand anything. The times when he wasn't what she needed him to be, Cat was left floundering. She had to shore up her own strength and figure out how to help on top of that.

She needed to do better. Be Stronger. On her own. But when she was so used to having strong men in her life, she had to face the fact she had taken it for granted. She'd failed to find her own strength, all too reliant on the fact they would always be there.

And in the next moment, her whole world rocked. Like when he'd been in the hospital.

Now it was happening again, all the worry that he would have to leave the police department. That something might happen, and he would never be the same again.

Simon said, "Although, if you're up to it maybe you could show us what happened."

"What do you mean?" Cat turned to him. "He was attacked." They were here to support Romeo. Why did it seem like Simon wanted to work the scene or something? "This is a police matter. Romeo needs to give a statement, and he needs to get checked out by a doctor. And not necessarily in that order."

Simon's expression shuttered, and he nodded to the side.

She stepped away with him, out of earshot of anyone. "What is it?"

"My program pinged." He still had his laptop under one arm, though he had the lid closed. "The address for this place showed up as a no go."

"Like warning people to stay away?" What was he getting at?

"Maybe." He shrugged.

Behind him, Cat spotted Peter talking to a police officer she didn't know.

Simon said, "We need to look inside."

"Okay. Do you think it's connected?"

"We need to find out."

Someone called out, "Cat!"

She spun to see her father making his way to the ambulance, using his cane to steady himself. Lately, it seemed like it was a fail-safe more than a necessity for him to use it. She tugged Simon's elbow toward her father, and when her dad came near enough, she gave him a hug, feeling the scratch of his cheek against hers. His shoulders were broader like Romeo's, and he carried the tension there.

"Hey." She gave him a quick squeeze and stepped back.

"Is he okay?"

"Looks like a nasty scratch on his head and a bump. He's a bit out of it."

"No, I'm not." Romeo passed her and hugged their dad. "Did you introduce him to Simon yet?"

"What?"

At the same time, her dad asked, "This is him?"

Simon's eyes widened. "Uh..." He cleared his throat and stuck out his hand. "Simon Olson."

Peter strode up beside him, as if drawn there by some mystical twin tractor beam. Her dad shook hands with Simon, then his brother, who said, "Peter Olson."

"The twins that work for Vanguard, right?"

They both nodded, simultaneously muttering, "Yes, sir."

Romeo just stood there, grinning like the spectacle was highly amusing to him.

"This is my father, Warren Alvarez," Cat said. "Dad was a police officer for thirty years."

He had retired with accolades, commendations, and a pension befitting a career of service. She smiled, glancing between the twins and her dad. Simon and Peter probably didn't consider it a good thing that her father had been in law enforcement.

"Don't worry." Romeo leaned over and clapped Simon on the shoulder. "None of us were there when Lucas took down your father."

Peter said, "Neither were we."

Cat reached over and shoved her brother's shoulder. "Dude!" She should slap him upside the head, but that wouldn't help the pain he was in. Sometimes, her brother could be such an idiot.

Her father gave him a chiding look. "Romeo." Dad shook his head.

"What?" Romeo glanced around.

"How about you tell us what happened?" Cat suggested. "Maybe we could go inside, and you can walk us through it."

It didn't take much convincing to get them all inside, and the final piece of the puzzle happened to be her father talking to the lieutenant on scene—Romeo's boss. Her brother didn't walk as fast as he usually did. Peter held the door for them.

A couple of officers glanced over. Someone, who was being held back, called out, "Peter!" He only lifted two fingers and kept going.

"You have groupies now?" Romeo quipped.

"Like you don't?" Peter grinned at her brother.

Simon glanced at Cat as they stepped from the street onto

the sidewalk in front of the neighborhood grocery store. Trash overflowed the can, and tied-up grocery sacks stuffed full sat on the ground beside it, along with fast food bags and empty cups with the lid and straw a few inches away.

As soon as they stepped in, Simon opened his laptop and folded it back on itself, so it resembled a tablet with the keyboard underneath.

She walked with Peter and Romeo.

"I was here. Getting some mints." Romeo stopped in the middle of the center aisle and turned around. He still probably needed to see a doctor. Despite that burst of energy, he wasn't all right. He might've been jazzed to see her dad or wanted to watch the first time Dad met Simon and his brother...but she could see the pain in his eyes.

She scanned for cameras. Simon ducked left, going into the neighboring aisle. His head extended over the top shelf as they were barely six feet high.

Romeo pointed at her or behind her at the shelves. "Something hit the back of my head." He looked around. "I don't see anything. Maybe whoever it was jumped up, reached over, and pistol-whipped me?"

Cat hissed.

"I hit the other side of the aisle and then the ground." He pointed at stock items scattered over the floor. Gum and mints had rolled everywhere, along with cough drops and pain medication bottles.

Peter said, "Someone attacked you out of the blue. You weren't responding to a call?"

"No." Romeo didn't shake his head. "I think I overheard someone talking. I need to think about it, but maybe someone was on the phone?" He turned and looked at the mirror up in the corner of the wall, an oversized circle with a warped reflection of Simon in the next aisle. "I looked...and then I don't know what happened."

"Got something," Simon called out.

Peter headed for him. She hesitated. Taking care of her brother in this moment was more important. "You need to get checked out."

"I'm fine." He might've been trying to whisper, but it came out louder than that.

"We both know that's not true." Cat studied his face, trying to get a read on how bad it was. He wasn't going to listen to her—she could see it—so she stepped back. "You put yourself and others at risk when you don't admit there's a problem."

Cat turned and spotted Peter looking at her, reflected in that warped mirror. She walked to the end of the aisle and found the twins.

Simon pointed to the floor. A cell phone. "It's one of them. This phone is on my network."

TWENTY

Simon took a step toward it. Peter smacked Simon's chest with the back of his hand. "It's evidence."

Cat said, "I'll grab an officer to collect it."

He didn't look at her as she walked away, but Peter would notice that the same way he'd notice if Simon had watched her go. His brother said, "So...she's great."

"Shut up."

Peter grinned.

"It's not like that."

"Maybe it should be."

Simon wasn't going to get into a debate about him and Cat when she was already headed back to join them, along with a uniformed officer. He and Peter moved down the aisle away from them.

Simon watched her then, trying not to be a stalker but there was a whole lot to appreciate about this woman. Her toned figure, not oddly stick thin like some women. She worked out, but she also came from a Hispanic background. She knew how to appreciate the fuel she put into her body—more than he'd ever learned how to do. Their father had even managed to warp their view of food, withholding it as a punishment.

He glanced at his brother. "Do you ever look at pizza and get like...an odd feeling in your stomach?"

She must've heard his question because he saw Cat glance over out of the corner of his eye.

Peter grinned. "That's a crying shame." The humor dissipated from his face pretty quickly. "Actually, for me, it's rice with little pieces of veggies in it. We got Chinese takeout, and Selena noticed. She made me tell her."

Simon could see how that might be a trigger. They'd eaten plenty of it as kids, and it was all wrapped up together in the swirling pit in his heart and mind. But it was the last thing Peter said that stuck with him. *She made me tell her.* "Jasper is forcing me to attend a trauma survivors group or I'll lose my job."

"So do it. Or don't and go earn four times as much with another private security company—or in a government job doing black site work into...whatever." Peter's face looked impassive on the surface, like he didn't care.

But Simon could see something very different in him. A whole lot of emotion. "I'm not leaving Vanguard."

Peter just stared. Finally, he nodded.

It honestly made Simon feel better knowing his brother shared a lot of his issues, those tendencies to have odd responses to what should be normal situations. Simon wanted his brother nearby but also didn't want to be an obstacle for Peter and Selena. His brother was probably excited that Simon would have someone like Cat in his life because he'd be a little more settled.

The officer collected the evidence, touching the phone with gloved fingers. They took so many photos of where it had been found that Simon's eyes flashed with white spots. Cat wrote on the bag with a Sharpie. "Thanks." She turned to them, holding the bag. "Do you need to connect to this phone?"

Simon shook his head. "Is it switched on?"

She touched the power button through the bag. "The screen is shattered. He must've dropped it." The screen remained black.

Simon shifted his laptop, tapped the power button, and used his fingerprint to wake up his device. He tapped the program. "Pete?"

"Yup." His brother didn't take the phone from Cat. All he did was hold the buttons in the sequence they'd come up with. The screen flashed green, like old computers used to do, and then their black screen came up with green text displaying the programming. He was young enough a lot of things about computers were retro.

Text scrolled down the phone.

Cat asked, "What did that do?"

Simon said, "Pretty much a factory reboot. It's just that I run the factory."

Peter chuckled. "Pretty sure you invented the whole company. Coming up with this? I'm guessing no one ever told you this thing is *genius*."

Simon hadn't explained it to anyone. He mostly tried to avoid the whole thing. After all, it had been something he was forced at gunpoint to figure out. That whole incident was wrapped in a bunch of messed up memories and fear that still lived in him, which hadn't been exorcised, and he didn't plan to do it in a group. Since then, the network had been used exclusively by criminals. He hadn't been able to shut it down or figure out who from the family was the person behind it.

"He's right, you know," Cat said. "Even if it was used for

evil, you still have to appreciate the fact you did something amazing."

She took a step toward him. Peter responded by turning and wandering away, and Simon ignored the why of it. "I'm going to get this where it needs to go, and then I'm going to make sure Romeo gets seen by a doctor. Do you need me for anything?"

Simon stared at her. *I can think of a few things.*

But now wasn't the time to be thinking about her full lips and how it would feel to kiss them. Even if it was an epically bad idea, he would likely still find it enjoyable. Too bad he tried to not be that guy these days. Lena had torn his heart to shreds. He refused to turn around and do the same thing to someone like Cat. Lena would deserve it, if revenge was his thing. Cat definitely did not.

She must've caught the look on his face and read something into it because she touched his cheek. Cat lifted up on her toes and kissed the other cheek. "Call me if you need anything."

Simon's cheeks heated.

She trailed out with the officer. A guy stepped in along with a couple of cops, one of whom was the on-scene lieutenant. The guy was probably in his fifties and wore wrinkled slacks and a Seattle NFL sweater. His short hair stuck up on one side as if he'd been sleeping on it.

Peter slapped Simon on the back. "Real slick...I was gonna say *Romeo* but that doesn't really apply now. That guy leaves broken hearts everywhere he goes."

"Hopefully, only one at a time."

Peter didn't get the chance to ask Simon what he meant because Simon just shrugged it off.

"Guys?" The lieutenant interrupted their silent exchange.

"Peter." He shook the cop's hand, then the plainclothes sleepy guy. "This is my brother, Simon."

"You guys are twins." The football fan glanced between them.

Neither of them confirmed what was completely obvious. The lieutenant said, "This is Max Kendall. He's the manager."

Peter asked, "Can you tell us who was working tonight?"

Simon needed access to the surveillance the store surely had to deter thieves. "And where your computer is?"

"There should be two girls working, but I need to check the schedule." Kendall led them to the back hall and a tiny office with wood wainscoting on the walls. He shook the mouse, then sat and woke up the computer. "Sarah and Becky should both be here."

He lifted the phone and dialed a number.

A cell rang elsewhere. Peter disappeared and came back with the ringing phone. Kendall hung up.

Peter said, "This was on the table in the break room."

"I'll try Becky."

No phones in the building rang. While Kendall talked to Becky, Simon waved him back from the computer. Simon had found the software they used to digitally record from the surveillance cameras and opened it. Four boxes on the screen gave him views of the inside of the store. One camera was behind a mirror. Another showed the cash register, perhaps to make sure employees weren't stealing. The third showed the cops out front on the sidewalk. The last one had an error symbol. The back doors?

Simon glanced at his brother. "One of the cameras is out."

Peter left the office.

Kendall set the phone down and looked at the lieutenant. "After I threatened to fire her, Becky told me Sarah clocks in for her. Becky was on her way—she went to a party first." His lips twisted. "Sarah is seventeen. She shouldn't be the only employee on the premises."

The lieutenant said, "There were no employees here when we showed up. And her phone was still here. We need to find her."

Simon said, "I'll pull up the feed and see where she went."

Peter walked back in while he scrolled back in time to see Sarah behind the register. "Camera out back is busted. Someone smashed it."

Kendall muttered something about unnecessary expense.

Simon hit play. Romeo walked down the aisle where he'd been looking for mints. And the man in the next one over watched him realize who was close by. The guy was on the phone. He pulled a gun and pistol-whipped Romeo over the top of the aisle. Then he hopped down, dropping the phone. He didn't bother to pick it up.

"He hit Officer Alvarez, dropped the phone, and ran for the girl. She'd sprinted to the back hall when he jumped up and smacked the cop." He had to refer to Cat's brother that way so that it left out their connection.

Kendall said, "Our employees are taught to run and hide after they hit the panic button under the counter. Which I'm not sure she did."

"She fled. He chased her," Simon said. "But we don't have footage of what happened after he followed her down the hall."

Peter said, "He could've been here to take her. If he knew she would be here alone, he could've been waiting to strike. Romeo was going to mess it up. Things were planned and in place, so he had to hit Romeo rather than just waiting until he left or risking that she would tell the uniformed officer that she was scared over something."

The lieutenant nodded. "We need to find her."

Peter asked, "Any idea who it was?"

Simon backed up the feed again, trying to get a view of the man. "Hoodie. Similar height as Romeo, but that's a rough estimate."

"Can you ID him?"

The lieutenant said, "You know the players?"

If only he didn't have to be connected to this at all, but he had to face reality. "Maybe."

"Is this the case everyone is working on?"

Simon nodded.

Peter said, "I'll run it down for you. Get you looped in."

"Thanks." The lieutenant rocked on his heels, then back to the balls of his feet. "This whole thing needs to be stopped." He eyed Kendall suspiciously. Did the lieutenant think the guy might be in on it or at least know enough to leave things at the store set up this way?

Probably not. He'd seemed genuinely concerned that one staff member had covered for the other and left the place with only one employee working that night.

"How many abductions does that make now?" The lieutenant glanced between them.

Simon swallowed. Peter would've said, but Simon needed to be the one to voice it aloud. "Five or six, at least. And we know this isn't the first time they've done it."

"Done what?" Kendall asked. "What are you talking about, abductions?"

There was no way to fake that kind of surprise. Oh, the lieutenant had asked just to see this man's reaction. He said, "If you'll come with me, Mr. Kendall. Your other employee should be arriving soon."

They trailed out, leaving Simon and Peter alone in the office.

"We need to stop this."

Simon didn't look at his brother. "We have no idea if they're done or if they are going to take more girls."

"So find out where this 'party' is going down." Peter rolled his shoulders. "Let me stop it before it happens."

Simon said, "I think we need to talk to Justice."

TWENTY-ONE

Cat gripped her phone while walking through the lobby. She still had a few minutes before Simon and Peter showed up. "That's a good idea, even if we have to wake up the household and drag Justice out of his bed. This thing is getting out of control."

Simon had told her how the employee at the store was the latest victim. It had been a couple of hours since she'd been abducted, maybe longer. The clock was rapidly approaching midnight, and they all needed sleep, but with innocent—and underage—girls at the mercy of a nightmare, Cat had no intention of going to sleep without at least some kind of result.

He might have given his brother the information for the estate where he'd been held, at least the area he'd been in, but they needed more. "Do you know where Justice lives?"

"Hang on." The background noise on the call changed. "I put you on speaker because I need to pull up what I found from the district network."

"You hacked the school computers?" She frowned.

"In about three minutes." Someone snorted, but it

might've been Peter. "The address listed isn't the same area as the estate, and his guardian is an aunt."

"So something happened to his parents?"

"Who knows? It's almost like the kid came out of nowhere. I don't know that the aunt is even real. I mean, she has social accounts and an address. She has a website for a freelance graphic design business, but if you dig at all, it starts to have gaps."

"Like a thin attempt at a fake person? Or some kind of fake ID passing as real?" Why would a guy like Justice need to hide his family? It could be that the family wanted him to have a normal high school experience, so no one knew Justice Spears wasn't his real name. He had to be connected somehow, given that Simon had seen a photo of him at the estate where he'd been held.

Cat stepped outside into the cooler night air. She had no sweater or jacket, and a badge and duty weapon weren't going to keep her warm even if they made her feel better.

She should go back inside until they actually pulled up so she wouldn't get cold out here. They weren't going to be more than a few minutes.

She turned back to the doors. A man stood behind her, far too close. She felt a tug at her hip from someone else. No, no, no! She shoved out with both hands and her phone at the person trying to take her gun from its holster.

Her palms glanced off a forearm. He had the gun already. She'd never seen him before.

The other one moved. It was happening to her. They were going to drug her and take her to this "party," subject her to the things Alayna had gone through. She was going to be...

He wrapped thick arms around her. Cat kicked her legs, but the struggle was useless. Her phone cracked on the sidewalk. The two men walked quickly to a car that pulled up at the curb. A shiny white SUV.

The back door opened. Someone shoved a cloth bag over her head, cutting off her vision so that all she could do was stare at the woven dark threads in front of her eyes.

She was tossed.

Cat hit the carpet on the floor, her back against something hard. The center console? She started to move away, and a baseball bat hit the side of her head. At least, that was what it felt like.

Punched. She'd been punched.

Cat didn't try to move after that. Hard, thin plastic wrapped around her wrists in front and was pulled tight before she could do anything that would enable her to break the ties later. The skin of her wrists met together in the middle at an odd angle. She sucked in a breath through her nose.

Doors closed, and she jumped at the volume of it. The vehicle revved, and they set off. Her body swayed with the turns, but she didn't bother to catch herself. Someone shifted their leg, so she leaned against it. She heard whispered conversation. Snatches of words that didn't mean anything with no context.

What do you want with me?

She still had her badge. They had her gun. No phone. She couldn't fight off multiple assailants in an enclosed space all at once. There could be more than two guys in here.

Cat prayed harder than she had in a long time—probably since Sergeant Ellis had been bleeding out. Dying in front of her.

Her breath hitched. *Lord.* She whispered a whole lot of things in her mind, not sure if any of them actually made sense. God knew. He listened to her heart. Even if she didn't feel all that close to Him, she knew He always listened to His children. It was why she'd continued to pray.

The car stopped. Her back shifted away from the hard plastic thing with knobs, and then she hit it again. Buttons jabbed her spine. Cat bit back a cry, pursed her lips, and let all the fear and rage and pain show on her face. Because no one saw it.

Only God knew what she couldn't hide from Him.

Doors opened, then closed.

Silence filled the vehicle—the absence of life. Then she heard the unmistakable sound of a gun being cocked. Cold washed over her.

No one removed the hood.

"Do not move."

His voice caused a shiver to roll over her. As if she'd been doused with an ice bucket.

"If you want to live and remain unharmed, you will sit there silent and listen to what I have to say."

She bit her lip to keep from making a sound. This guy was steeped in evil. In the quiet of her mind, she could say whatever, and he would never hear it. *I already know I don't like you.*

"Nod, if you understand."

She nodded. Her fingers had started to throb. Her wrists screamed with pain. The plastic ties were cutting into her skin.

"Very well." Silence seemed to reverberate against her ears before he continued, "There has been entirely too much attention from Vanguard and your police department on my business. I find it...unsettling to be the focus of so much attention."

Then don't be a criminal. Of course, she couldn't say that aloud. It might seem simple, but criminals didn't grasp the fact that if they didn't break the law, then the police and people like Vanguard would never worry about them.

"You are going to deliver a message for me to both of those parties."

This had to be the man that had abducted Simon. It had to be. She needed to get a look at him, but would he shoot her if she removed the hood? Yes, because that was exactly why she was wearing it. So that she had no chance of identifying him.

Like Simon.

"We are all going to live and let live."

Did that mean he would let *her* live? If she was the messenger, he had to keep her alive at least.

"Except for your friend Simon, who will receive the hand of justice soon enough for taking the life of one of my men."

Yeah, years ago. If only she could scream the words at him.

"I suppose you don't believe in an eye for an eye. And yet you attend church every Sunday. You read your Bible in the morning on your balcony."

Cat swallowed against the sick feeling that churned in her stomach. This guy had been watching her. He had someone spying on her. Maybe spying on all of them—even her parents.

"Do not test my resolve. My family will not be touched, and the life of my man will be avenged."

So why hadn't he done it already? It had been years. Why wait until now? *What do you want?* She needed to ask the question but didn't dare speak aloud.

"My business will continue. No lives lost. Just a little fun, and everyone goes home."

Was he talking about the "party"? She shifted, reacting to what he'd said before she could force herself to sit still.

"The girls are returned."

She couldn't stay silent. "You destroy them."

"And so, you'll volunteer to take the place of one?" he asked. "I would accept a trade. Are you prepared to save a single girl?"

Cat swallowed back bile. Could she do that, offer herself up instead of one of them? She was desperate to get them out. That was what they'd been working on.

But an exchange like that? It would destroy her just as it had done with Alayna and the others. Ruining what should be precious through degradation. The same way it would destroy the girl that she didn't take the place of.

Before she could answer, she heard the beginning of a low chuckle. It kept going but didn't increase in volume.

She made a face under the hood over his laughter, finding enough bravado to say, "You'll want to keep a tighter leash on Hayden."

The laughter stopped.

"If you want to stay under the radar."

"Any other sage advice?"

Cat said, "No, but I have a question." If they weren't going to kill her, and they weren't going to hurt her unless she offered to take a girl's place, then she might not lose much of anything asking. "Who killed my partner and shot me? I don't buy it was Arlo Wilson for a second."

"Interesting." He paused for several seconds and then asked, "You're bargaining with me?"

No, but would that get him to tell her? "If you want the police to...ignore you, then maybe offer something substantial in return for a free pass." As if she would actually give him one? The second she was out of here and free, she would tell the rest of the Benson PD *everything*. Problem was, what did she actually know?

The sound of his voice.

A hint of new car smell? It was safe to say he'd ruined that scent for her.

"I will give your offer some consideration."

Cat said, "Just do it. Call it a show of good faith."

She heard him knock on the window, a quick rap of his knuckles.

The door to her right opened and someone grabbed her elbow. Cat sucked in a breath. The person dragged her from the car. The plastic ties on her wrists cut deeper into her skin. She yelped and tried to get her feet under her.

Instead, one foot caught on the door, and she tumbled to the ground, landing on gravel on one knee before she planted her hands.

Doors shut. The car revved, and gravel peppered her as the car sped away.

Each sharp inhale and exhale filled the hood. A second later, she lifted her hands and ripped it off, snagging her hair in the process. Cat blinked at the trees around her, the shadows, the pitch-black parking lot with a hut—a detached structure that had a single yellow light above the door and a male bathroom sign. A moth buzzed at the glow.

She twisted around but saw no other cars. Not a single soul.

She had no idea where she was.

TWENTY-TWO

"Romeo, give me the phone." Warren Alvarez's voice sounded to Simon like he was in the background. A second later, there was a rustle, and then he asked, "You found her?"

No. Simon could say, *not yet*, but neither response came out of his mouth. "We're closing in."

That sounded like something Peter would say. Simon's brother drove the car, weaving through traffic on the freeway like this was Daytona. He hit a straightaway and peeled out ahead of the rest of the cars.

"How's that?" Cat's father needed reassurance, not a lengthy rundown of how Simon had hacked the traffic cameras outside the hospital. He'd found the vehicle they'd shoved her into with a hood over her head. She kicked and fought for her freedom. He followed the SUV across town to the exit Peter now took off the freeway.

"Sir, don't ask questions you don't want me to answer."

Her dad simply said, "You find her, son."

"I will." He hung up.

No way would Simon stop or even slow down. Cat was

out there. She had been taken by these monsters, and he was desperate to find her, the need overwhelming him as if he was hanging from the roof of a building by his fingertips, about to fall at any second. He would plummet to the street and lose everything.

That was what she felt like to him.

Everything.

"There." Peter hit the brakes. Up ahead on an empty highway lined by thirty-foot-tall pines on both sides was a two-lane road with a semitruck pulled over. The driver's door was open, and the light was on inside the cab. A man stood by the truck, gesturing. The woman looked at him, shaking her head and backing away.

Peter came mostly to a stop. Simon flipped the lock and climbed out, stumbling a little as he discarded all his things on the seat and avoided the door as he ran to her. "Cat!"

The driver spun around.

She looked terrified.

His footsteps ate up the asphalt between them. She was about to go down. He'd never run so hard in his life as he did that night, and a pain in his side sliced into his ribs. Simon blocked it all out—along with questions as to who this truck driver was and his intentions. He probably wanted to help the clearly distraught woman with her hands tied together wandering on the side of the road. The kind of person who would stop and help someone that needed it.

Simon said, "Thanks." It came out so breathy it almost wasn't audible. He ran right up to Cat. "Hey, hey." He touched her shoulders, and she flinched.

Eyes glassy. No blood. Maybe she'd hit her head.

He ran his hands down her arms, and she let out a whimper. Simon twisted around to find his brother right behind him. "Knife."

Peter dug in his pocket and unfolded a knife. Simon held her hands up to the light from the truck, and Peter cut her free.

She hissed out a breath. Blood had trickled from her wrists to wet her hands. The skin wasn't split all the way around, but the abrasions were deep, and in places, they were bad.

"Ambulance."

"Vanguard is quicker." Peter turned. "I'll tell her dad we found her. Sir!" He started to speak to the driver of the truck.

Simon tuned it out. She was the only thing that mattered. "I'm so glad we found you. Are you all right? Did they hurt you?" He touched her cheeks, sliding his fingers into her hair. "Cat, did they hurt you?"

She lifted her hands and gripped his forearms with more strength than he'd have thought she had in her right now. This woman was steel.

Her eyes still didn't quite focus. "Simon." She sounded relieved.

Hearing it made him want to thank God she was here and alive. So much he *almost* did it.

He opened his mouth to tell her they should go to the car when she shifted and moved close to him. Close enough that her body came flush against his, and her hands slid up his arms to his shoulders. She touched a sore spot on her wrists, and then her lips were on his.

Cat clung to him like she needed it.

Like she needed him.

Simon slid his arms around her and held some of her weight, so she didn't have to stand on her own strength. He held on to her and let her kiss him for as long as she needed it. It was for her, so she could feel grounded in that moment. So she could know to her soul that she had been found, that she was safe.

But hope crept in.

Slowly at first, like a whisper. Nearly a temptation—something he had a hard time with because of the way his father had warped so many things inside his head. But if there was anything to this hope, then it was her. *Everything.*

All of her was an invitation to something he'd never had. Even if he'd blown his chance at purity and it had all fallen apart, it still seemed as if he was being offered what he'd dreamed of in spite of all the ways he'd failed.

She kissed him because she needed it.

But in the end, he had to face the fact he needed it, too. He needed to be *needed*, and not in the way he had with his sibling, who would always be a part of him, but in a way that was Simon's and his alone. Catalina Alvarez was it for him.

She pulled away, breathless. Her arms lowered as if she didn't have the strength to hold them up any longer. He touched his forehead to hers and turned his face so their cheeks touched. "I've got you."

Her breath hitched, but he heard the audible sigh.

The semitruck was gone. Peter sat in the driver's seat of the car, still on the phone. He flashed the headlights, and Simon nodded. "We should go."

"Okay." She held on to him, and he would've offered to carry her, but she seemed like she walked well enough and wasn't about to fall.

Simon opened the back and ended up sliding in beside her like they had on the way to the grocery store where Romeo had been hurt. He buckled his seat belt, but she lay down with her head on his leg, curled on the seat.

Peter glanced at her, then Simon. "Good?"

"Yep. Hospital?"

Peter turned back to the front. "Vanguard." He pulled a U-turn.

Simon didn't argue or ask why. They had a paramedic on staff, and the doctor could be called. They didn't always have to go to the hospital, even if that was where her father and her brother were. Maybe Romeo was done getting checked out.

She had her eyes closed. Simon ran a finger over her hairline and saw her exhale. He prayed she fell asleep since the drive was over thirty minutes. For the first time in a long time, Simon acknowledged what he had always known to be true. God was real.

He wasn't the problem. God had never been the sticking point.

The issue had been the way others seemed intent to wield Him like a weapon. Like He was theirs to use to control others so they could feel as if they were in authority, the kind of people with all the power. And it was nonnegotiable for those with no power.

He'd never had to wonder if God was real or if His Word was the truth.

What he had to wrestle with was his own connection to that, what he was going to do with it, and how others factored in. He'd been ignoring the whole issue since his father died—maybe even before then. Now, while he asked for Cat to have peace and get some rest before she had to recount what had happened, there was a kind of clarity, with just him and God.

Soon enough, Peter pulled up to the curb in front of the building.

Not many lights were on in the tower, but there were enough to indicate more than a few people were here. Did she have it in her to face them? He never would have, but she probably could.

Peter opened the door. "I can carry her."

"She'll want to walk, but she needs a blanket." He touched her shoulder and started to shift at the same time. "Hey, sunshine. Time to wake up."

Why did he say that? Except right now, all the light they could find to fill the dark places and cast away the shadows was welcome.

She stirred, pushing up on one hand. "Ack."

"Let's get your wrists looked at." He helped her out of the car. "I'll be there every step of the way."

Peter closed the door and then rushed to hold the lobby doors for her. The elevator opened, and Violet held it. Blake was right behind her holding a blanket. "Come on. Everything is upstairs."

They rushed over as fast as Cat wanted to go. Simon took the blanket and settled it around her.

Violet had gloves in her other hand and tugged them on as the elevator doors slid open. In the harsh light overhead, Simon saw the state of her wrists.

Violet turned her arms so she could see all of it. "Okay, I've got just the stuff for this. We can take care of it, no problem."

She lifted her gaze to Cat, who stood in front of Simon so he couldn't see her face. If only he could tug her against him and slide his arms around her, if she wanted him to, but there wasn't time.

Violet asked, "Anything else we need to look at or talk about?"

Blake and Peter had stepped away from the two women about as far as they could get in the enclosed space. As soon as Violet asked, Cat took a half step back—which meant she slammed into him. He touched her waist.

She leaned against him. "They didn't hurt me."

Violet asked, "Aside from what I can see?"

Cat nodded. "I'm good."

His hand tightened reflexively on her waist. The elevator door opened, and they all spilled into the main office. It hit him then. This place that had been his sanctuary for years now. He'd brought Cat here so she could find peace in the place he'd found his so often.

When he needed it, and when he didn't know he did.

"Over here." He led her to his desk, beyond which a couple of armchairs rested by the windows. Something he and Destiny had come up with a few weeks ago. Kind of like a reading nook off to the side of all their cubicles. They worked long hours, and sometimes, a change of scenery helped.

She sank into the chair, and Violet sat on the edge of the table in front of her. Blake put a heavy duffel packed with medical supplies beside her.

Peter squeezed the side of Simon's neck where it met his shoulder. "Her dad is here."

Simon tore his eyes away from watching her get patched up and turned to see her dad and Romeo coming over from the elevator. Off to the side, where the hall led to Clare's—Jasper's—office, Blake stood with Destiny and Jasper, all of them in an intense conversation.

Cat's father made it to him, leaning heavily on his cane. "Son?"

Simon waited for the hammer to fall. *Stay away from her. This was your fault.* He braced for it.

Warren nodded. "Thank you."

TWENTY-THREE

"Thanks." Cat tossed the pills in her mouth and drank enough sips of water to get them down. Both her wrists were bandaged now, after Violet had slathered some gel cream on them. Maybe it would numb them. If only she could numb everything. Climb under all the blankets on her bed, where she could cover her head and pretend there was no fear.

Destiny shifted in the seat, not just because she was quite distinctly pregnant—something Cat wasn't going to point out. She wasn't an idiot. Besides, Destiny looked great. Happy. They'd explained all the connections. How Jasper and Blake had worked SWAT together at the Benson PD. She'd seen them and heard of them but hadn't met them.

Blake and Destiny were siblings.

Now Blake was married to Violet, and she'd come over from the fire department to work for Vanguard. Jasper had come from the PD also. Now he was the CEO of Vanguard, or COO. Or something that meant he ran the place. He was Simon's boss.

Destiny and Jasper were also married. Cat couldn't blame

the woman for looking so content being married to a man that good-looking.

Destiny asked, "Do you understand what I'm saying?"

Cat needed to write down everything that had happened. She needed to recount it out loud and have it recorded. What she didn't need to do was sit here and spend time talking about her feelings. That could come later, in her trauma group.

Cat nodded. "Thank you for sharing. That must have been a hard thing to go through."

Destiny blinked. She glanced at Violet. "That's...not why I shared."

"I know." Cat got up, even though pretty much everything ached. She went to the other armchair and patted Destiny's hand. "Thank you for telling me."

There were entirely too many people in the room. Cat needed to go somewhere else to have whatever breakdown she was about to have without anyone watching.

Her father sat on the edge of a desk in a tiny cubicle with no computer and no personal effects. His cane leaned against the side. He scanned her as she approached and then held his arms out.

"I'm okay." But she stepped in and took a moment to absorb the feel of her father's arms. Something she had always known but wouldn't always have.

"You will be." He patted her shoulder.

As soon as she stepped back, Romeo moved in. He tugged her to his side and kissed her forehead. "Hands hurt, or can you write?"

Better to just get it all out. "I'm good."

The words she and that man had spoken to each other rattled around in her brain as she did her best to hold on to them. She needed to get them onto paper so the others would know precisely what he'd said. They could use her statement to come up with a plan to catch him.

He handed her a pen and notepad.

Cat tugged out a chair and sat at someone's desk. *Simon.* The photos around the computer were of that police detective, his brother-in-law, wearing a suit standing next to a woman in a wedding gown—his sister. She looked a lot like him and Peter, enough that the resemblance was clear.

Another, much older, photo of a woman had been pinned beside it. The color was washed out, slightly orange. The woman had dark hair, fastened back, and a floral dress that was more than modest. She wasn't quite smiling. Behind her were palm trees and the door of a hut.

Cat moved his keyboard a little so she had enough room for the notebook. She described what she could remember of the two men. The hood. The car ride. How they'd stopped and she'd spoken with the man in the car.

She could hear his voice.

Cat flipped to another page and wrote down the snatches of the conversation she could remember, putting them in order as much as she could. She drew a couple of arrows and moved some around.

To her left, snatches of conversation floated around between Destiny and Violet, Jasper and Blake. Things like "...in denial. But it'll hit her."

Destiny thought she was pushing down what happened and she would fall apart later? So what if Cat did that? What happened when she was alone was between her and Jesus. Right now...she was a cop, and she needed to process this like a cop.

She'd fallen apart after they buried her partner.

After the funeral and the wake.

Around about midnight that night, alone in the shower,

she had sat there on the cold tile and cried for Ellis. For her own pain.

"We could get a counselor to come over." That was Jasper.

Cat wrote a couple more things, but she was losing focus.

Blake said, "We need her to tell us who it was."

"She didn't see his face." Violet was the one she'd told that to, in an effort to get across the fact he hadn't touched her. None of them had.

Cat closed her eyes. She could hear his voice, plain as day in her head, as if he were here. The same way they were talking.

"Maybe you should let her do her job." Romeo sounded irritated. "And quit talking about her like she's not here."

Violet said, "We're just concerned, that's all."

Cat opened her eyes. She'd written all she could remember right now, but it was a first draft at best. She'd need to compile it all into one statement where she could recount the conversation in order as much as she could remember.

They were all looking at her. She turned in her chair and found Peter and Simon on the other side, standing several feet away. She locked eyes with Simon and asked, "What if I can identify him by the sound of his voice?"

Simon came over. "I can find you a few samples, and you can listen to them. See if you recognize one."

"He only gave me warnings about the police leaving him alone. I tried to get him to give me something more, but it didn't work." This might, and then something good would come out of being taken. That it wasn't just about terrifying her. Using her as a pawn.

"It's worth a try." He tugged a different chair up beside her, and she gave him enough room. He typed faster than she'd ever seen anyone type.

"Wow."

The corner of his mouth curled up. She leaned back in his chair and watched his face while he worked. He'd sat pretty close and didn't seem to be concerned about her being in his personal space. Maybe he also hadn't minded the fact she'd ambush-kissed him earlier. It had been about the relief of seeing him, knowing she was safe and that the whole ordeal was finally over.

He'd accepted it. Maybe even enjoyed it.

He could've stepped away but didn't.

Right now, her brain felt pretty...addled was the only word she could come up with. That was a good word. She'd read it in a book recently.

Someone shook her shoulder. "Wakey-wakey." Romeo's face swam into view.

"I'm awake." She blinked. "Which means I need coffee."

Simon chuckled. "Okay. I have examples of four male family members, each of whom might be the man who..." The humor dissipated from his face.

Again, this would be easier if they were alone. He'd encountered the same ruthless man. "Are you sure you want to figure out who he is?"

Simon stared at her. It was probably hard for him to talk about it, but he was beginning to open up. The way a lot of people did when they were in a place that was safe for them to share. If he thought there would be no judgment here with his friends, she could accept that.

He swallowed. "When I'd reached the point that I could try to find out, I wasn't sure. Part of me didn't want to. It's harder to ignore what happened and pretend everything is fine when the specter has a face and a name. When he's a real person and I didn't stop him."

"You were seventeen."

He started to speak but didn't find the words.

She reached out and took his hand, linking their fingers. "No one faults you for surviving."

"I can fix it."

They would talk more about how, find out if he had a plan, but first, they needed to listen to these recordings he had pulled up. If they knew who it was, they could focus on how to take him down and find the girls. Stop the party.

He shifted the chair back. "I need to make a call. Let me know if you figure out who it is." He paused. "Actually, tell Peter."

Before she could ask if he was okay or just avoiding what she was about to, he'd walked away toward Peter. His brother only looked at him. The four people over by the armchairs had gone back to the conference room. They were giving her space. The moment she pinpointed the man's identity, they would be back here.

Romeo, Peter, and her father stood around her like sentries.

She looked at Peter. "I am okay right now. But I don't think Simon is."

His nose wrinkled. "He's tired. That's pretty normal."

Had he only said that because her father and brother were here, listening? If it was just the two of them, would he have told her something different? Life between them seemed to be a balance of what they knew about each other and what they were willing to share with the world.

Her mind started to wander. Thinking about meeting Selena. About sitting in her chairs with Simon, talking and looking at the stars. About sleep. A lot of sleep. It was nearly three in the morning, and they hadn't slept much the night before.

She clicked on the first video, then three seconds later, she shut it off. "Not him." She dragged that window to the left side monitor so it was out of the way.

The man in the next frame seemed familiar. "Who is..."

Her dad said, "I voted for that guy."

She winced. "Politics isn't really my thing. I try to care, but it seems like the whole thing is just backward." She hit play and prayed it wasn't this family member.

His voice was too squeaky. "It's not him." She moved that window over, too.

"You seem pretty sure." Romeo sat on the edge of the desk beside her.

"I hope I'm sure when, or if, it is him." She clicked the next one and immediately sucked in a breath. She pushed the chair back and stood, nearly falling.

Her father was there. Right behind her. She wasn't alone with this guy or his men. She was with people who cared about her.

She wasn't bleeding on the floor of a store, praying with everything in her that Sergeant Ellis would live. God hadn't shown up in that moment. Her partner had died.

She had lived.

His children had lost their father, and his wife her husband.

She had lived.

Why hadn't she realized that, in that moment, some piece of her trust in God had died with her partner? That she'd lost some of her childlike faith and died a little to the idea of hope and trust in a sovereign God?

Clearly, that's what had happened inside her heart. She'd been going through the motions ever since. In denial, pushing it down—like Simon often did. Making them more alike than she'd realized.

"This one?" Romeo pointed at the screen. Those in the

conference room came out. Her brother asked, "This is the man who abducted you?"

She stared at the screen. *Lance North.* Entrepreneur. Philanthropist. Beloved tech mogul, and staunch family man.

Cat nodded. "That's him. That's the guy."

Her father said, "This is gonna be a problem."

TWENTY-FOUR

"Lance North."

Simon heard the words behind him. He spun around in the tiny alcove at the end of the hall by the stairs. If he looked past Peter, he'd be able to see all the way down to Clare's office—Jasper's office.

Peter asked, "Who are you on the phone with?"

In his ear, Talia said, "Boy, you did not wake me up at three in the morning just to give me orders."

"T—" What else could he say? He'd told her what he wanted.

Peter snatched the phone from him and put it on speaker. "What did he ask you? He looks like that time I caught him transferring seized mob money out of federal accounts no one had touched in decades and into that children's hospital account."

Talia chuckled.

Simon couldn't find it amusing. *Lance North.* That was what Peter had said. Which meant Cat had identified him.

The police and Vanguard would go after him. Lance

would see them coming, and people Simon cared about would be targeted. The way Cat had been tonight.

He would never forget the look on her face when he found her. The relief on her dad's and her brother's faces when she showed up here.

No. No way was he going to let that happen again.

"Sie." Talia had her "mom" tone going on.

"You weren't asleep. You were online."

"The baby woke up, so I...checked a few things."

"I'm fine." His stomach tightened.

"But you want me to nuke it? Dump the whole program, shatter it to pieces so no one can ever put it back together again?"

Peter looked at him.

Simon clenched his back teeth. Yes, he had asked her to do that without telling Peter or asking Jasper for permission. "This is my mess. I'm the one who gets to decide how it's cleaned up."

What was the point in telling them when he could have it completed before the conversation ever would've finished? He and Talia could have taken it apart somehow, right? Brute force. Using the back door he'd programmed. It was time to be done burying his head in the sand about this thing.

Wasn't facing it what everyone wanted from him.

"Enough biding our time and waiting for some way to dismantle this organization or to get enough probable cause for a warrant." Simon took a breath. "I'm not doing that. He's done. This is over. We don't need the server location anymore."

Even without the man's name, he'd decided to take it all down.

Topple the empire.

Not just because he couldn't listen to the recordings and see her reaction to hearing the man's voice. She'd looked at Simon just now with innocent surprise. It should always be that way. She shouldn't have to ever think about how he put her in danger.

"We can keep her safe," Peter said.

The phone speaker rustled. "I think I need to meet this girl."

Simon asked her, "Are you going to help me dismantle it or not?"

"Kid, you know it doesn't work like that." Talia paused. "Even if we shatter it from the inside, he just puts it back up. Brute force doesn't solve the problem when he has the physical server the program is hosted on. He just reboots and starts all over again."

Simon gritted his teeth. "I have to do *something*."

"First thing, I'll pack up the kids and head over. Destiny set up that daycare yet? I heard she was callin' it Tactical Butterflies."

And risk someone else being in danger. "I don't want you here."

"Boy, don't nobody tell Talia what to do but Jesus."

And her husband, but neither he nor Peter said that. Talia and Mason were good people who had a solid relationship where respect went both ways. But they also had three kids. How could he let them put themselves in danger?

Things were bad enough already.

Talia said, "If you want my help, it happens in person."

"If you want to come here, get a helicopter and a security detail. Nothing less." Simon wasn't going to budge on this.

"I've got a whole federal taskforce, you know?"

"Yes, ma'am." Simon looked at his feet, his cheeks heating. "I need to get back to Cat." Especially if Talia wasn't going to help him do it now. Why did she need to come here? The fear that something would happen to Cat, or Talia and her family, tasted bitter on his tongue.

"I'll text you." The call ended.

Simon huffed out a breath. "Great, she sounded mad."

"What did you think was going to happen, bro?"

As if Simon needed to answer that question? "I want this to be over."

"Then let's go figure out how we're gonna do that."

It wasn't that easy. "That's what you've been waiting for?"

Peter stilled. "I couldn't do anything then. You didn't want to talk about it, and I didn't want to ask. I knew what you went through."

And at the same time, he didn't have a clue. Though, he knew now.

"Dad was on our case. Freya was doing what she could, but no one would ever have gotten through to you without breaking something inside you. And I wasn't prepared to do that."

Simon said, "I'm not prepared for that to happen now to anyone else."

"Then let me do this with you."

Jasper appeared in the hall behind Peter, down where this hall fed to the main area. "Briefing, now."

Simon pressed his lips together.

"He's a good guy and a good boss."

"He's not Clare."

Peter asked, "And you're going to complain about that every minute?"

"I don't have to think everything's great."

"You don't like change. That's what it is."

Simon trailed around his brother.

"Unless it's Cat." Peter followed behind him. "Then

you're up for all the change. And I can get on board with it if you do it right and treat her with respect."

"Agreed." Romeo stood by the wall with his arms folded. Everyone else had heard, or they seemed like they had. Maybe not Cat. Peter hadn't said it that loudly.

If only Simon could hit the elevator and make a run for it. They were all looking at him like they expected him to make a speech.

Simon looked at Cat. "We know who he is?"

In his mind, he heard a voice, low and full of authority. His vision obscured by the hood over his head. She'd been through it.

Now she knew.

"Lance North."

Jasper took up right where she left off. "Run him down. I want to know everything, all his business dealings. Property he owns where he might be having this 'party.' Full financials. Everything you can find out about his personal life."

Simon needed to get to work.

Romeo said, "I read Cat's statement. Given what she said to Lance about Hayden, we need to look for him. Try to find him before Lance does."

She gasped. "You think he's going to hurt him?"

Simon crossed the room, walking between cubicles to pull up a chair next to her. As he did, her father said, "You said what you needed to say to keep yourself alive."

She looked at her dad. "I didn't think he would hurt Hayden because of me. I was trying to get some good faith, exchange information and try to find out more about what he's up to."

"You can't bargain with a guy like that, Cat."

She winced, not looking at her father. "I just... I don't know. I was trying to stay alive. Like you said."

Simon took her hand. "Would every crime committed as a result of the communication network be my fault because I'm the one who created it?"

She blanched. "No, of course not. You don't have anything to do with them."

"That doesn't make me feel any less guilty." The fact was, he *had* made it. And then when he had the means to take it down, they'd been so far under the radar he hadn't seen a need. For all he'd known, it wasn't being used. He hadn't looked into it, preferring instead to ignore the whole ugly nightmare.

Years ago.

In the past.

Like the rest of his bad dreams that he tried to forget. But living only in the present hadn't ever done him any favors. He had his family, but not much else to show for it.

Romeo came over and kissed her forehead. "Peter and I will go find Hayden."

Cat frowned at her brother. "You're going to work with Vanguard now?"

"If it keeps my family safe." He strode out.

Jasper came over and stood near Cat's father. "Simon, what can you tell me about Lance North?"

Cat glanced at him.

Simon asked, "May I?" and motioned to his computer.

She slid her chair over. She was clearly still in some pain even if she'd taken whatever pills Violet had given her.

The notepad with her statement lay on the table. His gaze snagged on a couple of the words, but he forced his attention to the computer and pulled up what he'd already found. "I've been monitoring the family for a long time. Part of a group of people I keep an eye on. Bankers, tech moguls, politicians..." He spun around. "Oh, uh..."

Jasper shook his head. "We're good. I'm coming around to the idea of you...doing what you need to do."

Oh, boy. They needed to figure this out. Otherwise, they were barreling toward even more of a misunderstanding.

When this case was over, he and Jasper needed to figure out how to work together.

"Lance North owns a number of tech companies, including the media corporation that owns the Splurge shopping app, and he has a controlling stake in others. He owns investment firms and research firms, several of which tie to foundations that make him look lily-white on the surface, so his PR company has something to work with when things get sticky."

Cat said, "What about locally, in Benson?"

Simon found that part of his notes. "The entire chain of Wildmare Hotel and Suites."

"Those are everywhere."

"But if the girls are there, we have no way of figuring out which one. He has thirteen hotels. We can't search every room in every hotel. That would take forever."

"We could try." Cat shifted in her seat. "Can we get enough people together to do that?"

Her father said, "It would tip our hand, all that happening. He'll know we're onto him."

"But how can we narrow it down?"

Simon said, "Along with that chain, he also owns the Wildmare Spas up in the hills north and southwest of here."

"I've been to one with my mom." She sighed. "That sucks. Those places are nice."

Simon's mind was still spinning on the issue of how to narrow it down. Was there a way to find out if the girls had been brought to one of those places? Or if someone had seen one of them? Maybe he could call Bob and ask what was the best way to investigate this kind of thing.

"What are you thinking?" Jasper asked.

Simon glanced over. "How do we find out where they were taken?" He didn't mention that he might ask Bob.

"You don't trust cops, do you?"

Simon flinched. "Since when?"

"Just a hunch." Jasper stared at him, way too intently.

Simon glanced at Cat's dad, then at Cat. "When have I ever given the impression I don't trust cops? Lucas is great. Talia is a fed, and she's like...my best friend at this point."

Jasper just stared at him. His phone started to ring. "Hollingsworth." His expression darkened. "Got it." He hung up.

At least they'd get a change of subject. But this probably wasn't good.

"We were too late," Jasper said. "Hayden was dumped in front of the police department five minutes ago. He's dead."

TWENTY-FIVE

"How did he die?" Cat's stomach sank. She was so far past exhausted at this point that she was starting to get hungry. She'd never even met this Hayden person, but she should have some compassion that he no longer breathed.

Jasper said, "Three shots, center mass. The gun was handed over with his body, so they'll be able to run ballistics tests on it."

Cat spoke before she even thought it through. "And if it matches the round that killed my partner?"

"Then you'll be a step closer." Simon looked at her, but she didn't return the gesture.

Her cheeks heated. She was far too aware of their attention on her, so she looked at her father. He would always be her safe place to land. "Arlo didn't do it."

His jaw flexed, and she couldn't read his expression. "So find out who *did*."

She'd been trying to do that for years and gotten nowhere so far. Until a man was killed and turned over to the police. Definitely a statement, leaving a man dead on the doorstep of the police department with the weapon that killed him.

"He thinks he's doing us a favor." And she was the one who'd set it up to happen. Not exactly encouraging it, but she'd told him Hayden was a loose end. Evidently, loose ends got cut. "He killed Hayden to drop the low-hanging fruit so we wouldn't use the guy against him. Now he's free to do what he wants—or he thinks he is. He probably thinks we've been placated into backing off and giving him free rein."

Simon touched her shoulder. "It isn't your fault."

So he'd read what she'd put in the statement. "I offered him up."

"It's not on you."

They had already covered this. But tell that to her heart.

Her father pushed off the desk and stood, steadying his cane under him. "I need to go home to your mother."

She heard what he didn't say. That he needed to ensure her mom was all right and to ease her mom's fears if she was worried. Cat stood and gave him a kiss on his cheek. "Thanks for coming."

He sort of grunted, which meant "You're welcome" and "I love you" and also "Solve the case without getting killed so I can rest more easily at night."

She watched him go, then realized everyone was still looking at her. She turned to Simon, finding solace in the connection that was theirs alone. "We need to find Justice. They could be midparty right now, and we need a shot at saving some of these girls from what they might be going through. At the least, he could answer a whole lot of questions."

Justice could even be the one who had shot Hayden.

She'd tried to put him in the store when Ellis had been shot, but that was a few years ago. Not only would she end up warping her memory so that her testimony would be suspect, but the kid would've also been barely fifteen then. The shooter had been older than that. She thought so, anyway.

Simon turned to his computer. "I can run a trace on his regular cell phone. Find out what tower it's pinging off and where GPS puts him."

She moved to stand behind his chair. "Maybe it's near one of the hotels or the spa."

Would they get a result that easily?

They might. Perhaps God's favor would shine on their efforts, and they would bring down a bad guy. Save lives. Prevent awful things from happening.

It was why she'd become a cop in the first place.

I trust You. She couldn't affect the outcome more than what was in her power to do. Beyond that was up to God, which would prove scary if she sat and contemplated it. But that wasn't a bad thing. She had to trust Him, or what did her faith accomplish?

Things happened and she couldn't prevent pain or death.

Cat either trusted God had a plan or not. She either leaned on Him for the outcome—that she might not understand but which would be His best—or she had to walk away from her faith because it was meaningless.

Jasper said, "I'll call Russ and get the PD to wake up a judge. We'll get a warrant for Justice Spears's phone."

It would be out of order, given Simon probably had the information already. He definitely would before the judge signed off on the warrant to run his phone. She settled into the chair beside Simon. "What else can we find out so that when the warrant comes through, we're ready to move?"

He glanced over, an amused expression on his face. "Yeah?"

She should roll her eyes, but the dull ache in her wrists

and how she got the injuries dampened everything. "Fine. You could say I'm coming around to the idea."

Simon grinned. There was a very *come to the dark side* look on his face. Then he turned back to his computer, and it was almost like a switch was flipped. His attention was sucked into what he was doing. She probably could've tugged on the end of a longer lock of his hair and not have him notice. Or he'd have swatted at the annoyance like it was a fly.

Jasper paced the wall in front of them, walking to the window, and then back toward the wall at right angles from him, the conference room door, and the bank of elevators. He spoke into his phone as he paced back and forth.

Simon's fingers flew across the keyboard, faster than she'd have thought possible if a person wanted to type with any kind of accuracy.

She eased down in the chair, leaning her head back. Her eyes drifted closed, and it didn't take long before she was lulled into an exhausted slumber, accompanied by the rhythmic sound of the low conversation.

How long had she slept before Simon gently shook her shoulder? "Sorry. You should sleep, but you'll want to hear this."

Outside the bank of windows, the sky remained dark, and the clouds obscured her view of the stars. Cat sucked in a breath through her nose and blinked awake, trying to clear the cobwebs from her mind.

"We have him."

She pushed the chair back and stood, stretching. The ache in her wrists was back. She raised her arms above her head anyway and stretched left, then right. She caught Simon eyeing her and then the blush on his cheeks. "Coffee, and let's go."

Simon stood, gathering his laptop and sliding it in his backpack. "Just like that."

Jasper strode down the aisle toward them. "It's a cop thing."

Cat tapped a finger on her lower lip. "Probably doctors do the same thing. And soldiers. Not just cops."

Jasper shot her a look as if he didn't want to believe that. He wanted PD officers to be unique rather than part of a subset of people. He seemed to brush off the sentiment. "We're loading up and rolling out." He started to turn, then paused. "And the two of you are staying in the surveillance van."

Simon nodded.

Cat didn't argue, even though it crossed her mind. She needed more brain power than just having woken up to formulate an argument as to why she was going to be in on this...raid? Whatever it was.

He slid his backpack on and reached for her hand.

Staying in the van with him wasn't going to be so bad.

They climbed in with a guy driving that Cat hadn't met before. She buckled up on the bench seat in the back. "Where are we headed?"

Simon pulled his laptop out to set on his lap. Across from them was a table and full computer setup, like a mini–control room with a stool. In the corner was a stack of protective vests, a baseball bat, and a shotgun, beside which was a crate she didn't dare look in. Vanguard was serious. And now that she knew Simon and had met some of the others, she could appreciate the job they did a little more.

Even if, at the same time, the normalcy of her day job sounded like heaven.

Simon said, "The spa. One of them, anyway." He pointed to it on his map.

"That's where Justice is now?"

"His phone, at least." Simon nodded.

"Seems odd for a teenager who should be at school in the morning to be spending the night in a day spa."

"That's what we were thinking." He paused. "It's actually his birthday."

Cat frowned.

"His real one. All the information he gave to the school district is fake. His real name is Christopher Elliot North. He's Lance's nephew. We can't find any information for his parents. The mother isn't listed anywhere. The father is a North sibling of Lance's who has dropped off the map as far as we can figure. Jasper thinks Lance is raising him."

"Why wouldn't he publicize that? Show people what a great guy he is, taking on his nephew."

Simon shrugged. "We should ask that when he gets arrested."

Cat smiled.

"The FBI is on scene already. They've been working the girls' disappearances since Marianna Barker was taken, so they're all-in to help get them back."

"You know people at the FBI?"

Simon smiled. "They're pretty great. Law enforcement is a small world. They've had some turnover, but the core crew is solid. Benson is a great place to work."

"What about travel?" He didn't seem like the type of guy who took a whole lot of vacations, even though he had told everyone he was backpacking in Wyoming this week.

"Depends." He eyed her. "Are you coming with me?"

Before she could figure out how to answer that, the van came to a stop. The view out the front window was dark, maybe some trees. The driver got out and slammed the door.

"He'll keep watch outside, so don't worry."

"I wasn't," she said. "But now I kind of am."

Simon leaned over so his face was close to hers. "I'll keep you safe. You keep me safe. We can watch each other's backs."

Hmm. Was he usually alone in the van? "Sounds good."

He touched his lips to hers. So gentle. There and gone in a second, like a blink-and-you'll-miss-it experience. Then he settled on the stool and hit the power button on the control center, sliding an earpiece in. "Zero-One, ready."

She watched the system come to life. A map of the complex displaying red dots, probably the Vanguard people. Cat peered closely at the layout of the building, trying to work out where the girls might be held if they were here.

"Copy that." Simon glanced at her. "They're moving in."

She nodded. The red dots moved in simultaneously, a practiced operation. "Is Peter in there?"

"And Romeo, plus the FBI and a Vanguard team that works on the west coast, covering California all the way up to Alaska. They were helping the Royal Canadian Mounted Police a few months ago when all that craziness went down with the terror threat, and I think they're mad now because they couldn't help with it."

"Vanguard seems to have a lot of teams."

"It's a dangerous world."

"You're right," she said. "It is."

And when she didn't trust in the sovereignty of God, she would leave herself open to being swallowed up by the hopelessness of it all. She *had* to cling to Him.

Or what was she trusting in?

TWENTY-SIX

Simon had never had a woman in the van with him. In fact, there usually wasn't anyone with him in the van.

Through the earpiece, he could hear the team conversing with one another. Clearing hallways. Searching rooms. The report of gunfire made him jump, and for the first time in a long time, he prayed for his friends and coworkers that they would be safe. Guarded by God's power.

As far as he was concerned, God being God meant He could do what He wanted. Simon just needed to make sure he had done everything he could on their behalf.

Had Peter been praying for him? That would explain the change of heart. It could only have been a God-thing that Simon's feelings had changed in the last few days.

He muted his speaker. "Sorry, I can't turn the earpiece off. The computer doesn't have speakers, so the only way to hear what's going on is to wear the headset."

She smiled. "It's fine. You could update me if something happens."

"I can do that." He reached over and squeezed her knee.

"Have you heard from your parents since your dad got home?"

Cat slid out her phone. "He arrived home—I get alerts, and I can look up where he is. He also sent a message that they're both good and he's locking up. Setting the alarm."

"Good." Simon paused to listen. The FBI agent in charge of their team for this mission had found a staff member, a security guard.

"What did Peter and Romeo do last night?" she asked.

"When they didn't need to look for Hayden, the two of them kicked some doors in during the night. I don't even know who all they dragged out of bed to answer questions."

Cat shook her head. "That boy."

Simon chuckled. "A little more suited to Vanguard than most cops?"

"Geez, don't tell him that. I don't think he even realizes it. He'll swear up and down he's true blue to the core."

"I think maybe you are...more than him. If we're comparing." Simon said it carefully, not sure how she would respond to the statement. His attention shifted to the comms channel for a second. They hadn't gained any information from the security guard, who refused to talk.

She asked, "You really think so?"

Simon glanced at her and nodded, all he had time for before he said, "Copy that." To Cat, he said, "They're still working through the rooms, but the back side of the spa has several cars in the parking lot. More than should be there overnight. They're taking a look at the last few hallways."

Cat bit her lip. "I'm praying they find those girls."

"I'd have thought they would encounter a lot more resistance than they have. But maybe that's a good thing."

"They might purposely keep it low-key. All the girls are drugged, and it's invite only."

Simon winced.

"Yeah."

"I'm praying they're all here. Otherwise, we'll have more work to do to shut them down."

"Anything on Lance North? Do you think he's here?"

Good question. Jasper had asked Russ to work out a search warrant, but the judge hadn't signed off on that one. Perhaps all they'd done was tip off North that they were looking at him. "He doesn't have a normal cell phone that I can find. He might use one that's on my network, or he might have a business one I can't get the information for. While you were asleep, I tried to get into the company network. His email responses come from his assistant, not actually him."

"He doesn't stoop low enough to send his own emails." Cat made a face.

Her expression was adorable. "I don't even want to be the head of a department."

"What about teaching? You haven't done it for long, but you seem good at it."

Simon had been thinking about that as well. "I'm going to finish what I started and get the Algebra 2 kids through their summer semester. All in all, we've only missed a day and a half with the bomb threat. We should be able to finish it out."

Cat smiled at him. "I think that's great. Younger teachers always seem to connect better with the students, and everyone needs a solid male role model."

"I only know that's true because I never had one." Simon tracked the red dots as they closed in on the rear section of the building. He pulled up the schematics. There was a lower level back there, probably storage rooms. Simon flipped his earpiece mic back on. "One-One, this is Zero-One. Come in."

"Go ahead." Jasper sounded breathy.

"There's a lower level where you are, a floor below ground."

"Copy that. But where's the door? I don't see anything with stairs."

Simon scanned the blueprint drawing. "Looks like an elevator at the end of the hall beside a linen closet." Bigger than any cupboard for towels he'd ever seen. "The northeast corner."

"Copy that."

Gunfire echoed through the earpiece. The point where they'd start saying things like, "Encountering resistance" and giving each other locations so they could back one another up. Another shot rang out, followed by two more.

It sounded different.

Cat flinched in her seat and turned to look at the side of the van. "That was outside."

Simon flushed cold. "The Vanguard operative out there protecting us?"

"Did someone just kill him?" She drew her pistol and checked it, confirming there was a round in the chamber and flicking the safety on and then off again. The shift in her to *ready* was visible in the way she became steady, her lips pressed together.

The woman who cared about people enough to stop and ensure they had what they needed—even if it was only a soda and a comfy chair in the dark—disappeared, and the cop overtook everything.

Instinct. Training.

He'd seen it enough in Peter to know what was happening with Cat.

She would guard him with her life.

Someone tugged on the handle of the back door. Simon stiffened. "What are we—"

"We don't know how many are out there." She scrambled between the seats and turned the key, so the engine came to life. "Whoa. More than one, that's for sure." She shoved the van into gear, then lifted her gun and pointed it at the passenger's window.

She hit the gas.

The van jerked forward.

Simon nearly slid off the stool. Calls of "Found one" and "They're here" over his earpiece indicated the team in the spa had discovered the girls. Some, or all of them. Gunshots echoed over the comms channel.

A bullet splintered the van's back window but didn't shatter it thanks to the wire crisscrossed in the glass.

"Hang on! I'm getting us out of here."

Simon gripped the edge of the desk so he could hang on, literally. Was the man who'd been covering them outside dead? He had to be, given the way someone was still shooting at the back of the van.

Rounds pinged off the back doors and the sides as Cat gunned it away from the spot where they'd parked. "How many are there?"

"More than three, less than ten."

He'd have said a handful. Simon slid out his phone and sent an update to Peter. No need for anything to go awry in the spa just because they were worried about him and Cat. As long as they stayed ahead of their pursuers, they'd be okay.

"Where are you taking us?"

She gripped the wheel, the gun in her other hand. "To the spa. Safety in numbers."

"Copy that." The gunbattle over comms might actually be worse than the situation he and Cat were in. "Any idea who they are?"

No one had thought these people would go down easily.

But they should be attacking the invading men with guns, not the van.

A shiver went through him, and for a second, he was back on that cold concrete floor, seventeen and all alone. At the mercy of what they wanted. And their threats.

"No idea." She didn't sound irritated, just focused. "Hold on." Cat yanked the wheel to the side, and he held on while they careened around a corner. The tires bumped up onto asphalt, and the ride got a whole lot smoother.

Lord. What should he say?

Peter hadn't replied yet.

The team would see them hurtling down the lane up to the spa with the gunmen in pursuit. But it wouldn't hurt to make sure. Simon got on the radio. "All positions, this is Zero-One. We are approaching the front of the building while being pursued by armed assailants. Assistance required."

"Copy that." It sounded like Jasper. "On our way."

Jasper gave a series of orders, splitting the team between continuing the search and breaking off to help back them up. Hopefully, it wouldn't interfere with their operation. A few red dots moved away from the collection of the others. A few more were scattered throughout the building.

Cat hit the button for her window.

The van slowed, and she turned, brought her gun arm around, and squeezed off shots. Two. Three. Four. Would she empty her clip?

Her body jerked, and she slumped back, leaning over the emergency break between the front seats. The van continued to roll forward.

"Cat!" He scrambled toward her.

The doors opened behind him, but Simon ignored them. Blood. Where was the blood on her? She'd already been injured. She didn't need this.

"Freeze!"

He didn't listen. Simon turned her shoulders and saw a gaping wound bleeding badly, high on her right arm.

Someone grabbed the back of his belt.

He lost his balance and landed on his back on the metal floor of the van. A gun barrel settled in front of his face. It was all he could see. A low voice said, "You're coming with us."

"No—"

The gun came down and slammed into his temple. Pain exploded as his skull slammed between the metal floor of the van and the solid metal of the gun.

"You're coming with us." The man grabbed his shirt and used it as leverage to get a grip on Simon and slide him across the floor. He tossed Simon through the air. Out of the van.

He landed on his back on the asphalt and cried out.

Stars blinked overhead. He saw stars. *Cat.* She wasn't dead. She couldn't be. It had only been an arm wound, right? The van continued to roll slowly away from him.

"Get him in the car."

They hauled Simon up. He couldn't control his limbs, even while his mind screamed at them. There was nothing he could do to fight it. He had no power to stop them. He landed on the scratchy carpet of the trunk.

The lid slammed over him.

Under him, the vehicle revved, and they set off. His body rolled against the side. *Lord.* This time, he did know what to say.

Help.

He needed a way for Peter to find him. Simon shifted, which hurt a lot in the enclosed space. He had plenty of bruises by now, but they weren't worse than the gunshot Cat had suffered. At least she wasn't in here with him.

He dug out his phone to call Peter and...

The screen was shattered.
He hit the power button.
Nothing happened.
It was dead, and most likely, so was he.

TWENTY-SEVEN

Cat sat up, reaching for the steering wheel to pull herself up. She cried out. The door behind her opened.

"Cat!"

Thankfully, she wasn't about to get killed. That was a friendly voice, and it belonged to her brother.

"Hold on. I'll get you out." He grabbed her under the arms and dragged her back over the passenger's seat in front and out the door, where he set her on her feet.

The world swam around her, and she grabbed onto his arm with her good hand, letting out another cry.

"We'll get you looked at." He stared down at her with a dark expression. "There's about to be a whole lot of EMTs here."

She needed to see...

Cat used the side of the van for support and picked her way to the back doors. They were open. No one was inside.

She didn't see blood. She hadn't heard shots after she was hit, but she had heard a car engine. "They took him."

Peter ran up to her, and Romeo closed in. Simon's brother asked, "Where is he?"

Two more Vanguard operatives ran up to them, including Jasper and a woman she didn't recognize. The woman had long blonde hair tied back in a ponytail, and she wore a tank top and jeans. She had seriously toned biceps. Both of them looked worried, though Peter's expression was more like tortured.

"I don't know where Simon is."

Jasper looked at her arm, then reached into the van and came back with a duffel. "Sit on the edge."

She took a seat in the doorway, and he tore open a square of gauze. He held it against her arm and said, "Tell me what happened."

Cat swallowed down the bile that threatened to interrupt her attempt at telling the story. When the danger of that had passed, she said, "We were shot at. I think your guy, who was outside the van, was killed, but I'm not sure."

Jasper glanced at the woman.

She nodded, and a strand of blonde hair came loose from her ponytail. "I'll go look."

Cat watched her rush off.

"He's a friend of hers." Jasper replaced the gauze with another clean one. "Looks like a nasty graze. You might even need stitches."

"I need to find Simon."

Peter and Romeo glanced at each other. Both shifted their stances.

"I *am* going to find him."

Jasper said, "How many were there?"

Cat squinted at them. They had looks on their faces like they were about to leave her and go finish this themselves. If they wanted to do that, then why didn't they just leave already?

"Cat," her brother prompted.

She glanced at him and noted the serious freak-out going on behind his attempt at a blank expression. "Not less than three, not more than five. One car. Not an SUV. It was low down."

At least she wasn't in critical condition, hanging by a thread, and he had no idea. Yet again, she'd been unable to help. Someone she cared about was in danger, and instead of being at work and not getting the news, she'd been injured and still couldn't stop it.

Now Simon was in the hands of their enemy. He had been taken, and even though he'd escaped last time, it didn't mean he would find the opportunity to do so again. They had to find him. Rescue him.

But where were they supposed to start?

Did her brother and Simon's brother think she had the answer?

She shook her head and tried to focus. Jasper grabbed a bandage and wound it around her arm gently. "What happened after they showed up?"

"We heard shots outside the van. I jumped into the front seat, and they shot at us while I drove up here as fast as I could."

"Good decision." Jasper nodded.

It wasn't as though she'd actually been thinking, though. She'd been blind to any semblance of logic or working out a good plan. Panic. Instinct. Thankfully, her training had kicked in, and she'd headed for backup. It had been that or she'd have driven all the way back to Benson.

No contest.

"They grabbed him and took him. At least, that's what I

think I heard." She fought to retrieve the memories. "It must have been North's men, right? They need him to do something?"

If they didn't need Simon alive, they would probably have killed him here, moments ago.

Now she really was going to throw up.

Jasper glanced at Peter. "Surveillance on this place."

Peter nodded. "I'll find out if the cameras were on outside. Everything else was off, but something might have been missed. Maybe we can get a shot of the car."

Cat pressed her lips together to keep from mentioning how that was a serious long shot.

Peter turned and jogged for the front door of the spa. Jasper taped down the bandage and said, "That'll hold it for now."

He took a step away and Romeo took his place. "We'll get you a ride. I want you to go to Mom and Dad's place. Stay there, stay safe, and I'll call as soon as we find Simon."

Cat frowned. Stay there? Be safe and pretend Simon wasn't scared for his life somewhere. That he wasn't back in his nightmare. Romeo wanted her to sit on her hands and let him find the man *she* cared about. When he was free and all right—because she was the one who was going to find him— she would think about how she really felt. The fact that Simon Olson was a man she could love.

A man she might want to spend the rest of her life with.

"Don't argue with me, Cat." Romeo stepped back. "I'm going to help Peter. He and I have got this." He slapped a hand on his chest. "Let us take care of it."

He strode away.

Jasper had done the same, talking to the blonde. Her friend was dead—Cat could see it on her face.

No way could Cat convince her brother to let her help

him and Peter. They didn't want her to get hurt, thus trying to convince them to include her would be a waste of time and energy that she could put toward helping Simon instead. No point arguing when her brother was as stubborn as her. They wouldn't let her help? She would just work the problem herself.

She got up, turned, and looked into the van.

There could be something in the stuff here that would indicate how to find him. Or a message he'd left. No, that was unlikely. But would he be able to reach out?

Would he have access to the communication network he'd built wherever they took him? Maybe if she somehow got one of the phones he'd been tracking, she could connect with him.

Another unlikely scenario.

But she had to try something, and right now, anything was worth it if it could be the thing that got him back.

I need a way, Lord. Help me to figure this out.

But in the end, she had to make peace with losing him. She had to accept that God was still good even if she never got Simon back. If he was lost forever from his family. She had barely begun a relationship with him, and yet, she would grieve deeply. She couldn't imagine how Simon's twin and his sister, plus the rest of their family, were going to feel the depth of their loss.

A tall woman with short, cropped hair and FBI on her vest strode out of the front doors. Earpiece in. Gun in a holster on her belt. But it wasn't the woman who caught Cat's eye, it was the young man who walked in front of her.

She started toward them.

A helicopter buzzed over the spa's main building. Life Flight. They landed behind the building, which had to either be an open space big enough to accommodate them or an actual helicopter landing pad. Not that surprising, considering the spa catered to that kind of clientele.

Justice Spears spotted her coming, and his face twisted into a sneer.

"Sorry that we ruined your birthday party."

The FBI agent's eyes widened a little in amusement.

Justice had a glassy expression, and he didn't seem to be able to fully focus. "I want my lawyer."

"I bet you do. Thing is, this isn't my case, so I don't care about whatever charges you're facing. I just want to know who took Simon and where they would've taken him."

"Who?" Justice shrugged.

"Mr. Norris. Your math teacher. Guess what, kid. He was spying on you the whole time." That was satisfying to tell him.

Justice said, "You lie."

"I don't lie about the school. That would make me a bad Resource Officer." She went to fold her arms and nearly passed out. *Distracted.* She'd been shot before and could honestly say this time wasn't that bad. But being shot was never good.

Cat said, "Where is the family estate?"

"How should I know?"

"So you're just a wannabe? A hanger-on. Can't get rid of the kid, throw him a bone once in a while. Or a party."

He huffed. "They need me."

"Where can I find Lance?"

Justice shuddered. "You don't find Lance. Lance finds you."

"Right."

The agent shifted. Obviously, she was gearing up to cut off the conversation. There wasn't much time left to get information that counted.

"Justice, who killed my partner, Sergeant Ellis?"

His lips peeled back into another sneer. "That was a good one." He started to chuckle, turning far enough that she saw a phone in his back pocket. The FBI would confiscate that soon enough, but was it his personal phone or one of the devices Simon had identified?

Justice said, "Hayden's lucky day."

"What are you talking about?"

"There was a price on his head, so Hayden didn't hesitate. He did what he needed to do, and he got *paid*."

"And when you grow up, you wanna be just like him?" Cat challenged. "He's dead."

The FBI agent snorted. "If he says anything else, I'll call you?"

Cat said, "Alvarez."

"Got it." She walked Justice past Cat.

Cat reached out with her good arm and slid his phone out of his back pocket. If he noticed, he said nothing. She tucked the phone against the front of her shirt and walked fast to the corner of the building.

She stood in the shadows and hit the power button. The screen lit up. Definitely not his personal phone because what teenager used a simple black background? But how would she get past his code?

She needed someone who could access the system.

Peter.

No. She needed someone who hadn't dismissed her help and would *absolutely* want to be in the loop. Cat tugged out her own cell phone and opened the browser. How was she supposed to find the number that would get Simon's friend on the phone?

She typed *Talia* and *Northwest Counter-Terrorism Task-force* and prayed this would work.

Otherwise, she might never see Simon again.

TWENTY-EIGHT

"Come on."

They hadn't put a hood over his head this time. That was the first clue that Simon was going to die.

No way would they let him see this location and everyone's face without ensuring he couldn't lead the police to them later. Which meant that the only way he was leaving this place would be in a body bag.

The man grabbed his arm and dragged him from the car toward an electric car. Simon looked around, attempting to imprint it all on his memory. Concrete walls. Cars lined up in rows to the right and left. A collector's dream showroom.

In the center in front of them was a tunnel. Behind, where they'd pulled into this industrial-looking garage—the size of a football stadium—was a gated entrance. A motor whirred, and the gates eased shut, meeting in the middle. Then, a door rolled down in front of them, on the outside.

Completely disguising the entrance.

He didn't even know what it looked like on the outside as he'd been in the trunk for that part of the journey.

The rear door of the electric car was opened for him. Someone shoved Simon's head down. He forced himself not to react to being shoved around and slid in. A man slid in right behind him. Another got in on the other side, sandwiching him in the middle seat.

No one put a seat belt on. No one got out their phone and started to play a game.

The one most likely in charge got in the driver's seat, and the car accelerated with an odd electronic whir down the concrete tunnel.

The car was washed in pitch black. The occasional overhead light flashed through the sunroof, and the headlights lit up far too little of the road ahead of them. Just concrete and darkness. More concrete. More darkness. A long, straight tunnel of nothing.

This must be the place he'd been brought before. So familiar.

They drove for... It must've been miles and miles. Maybe seven minutes. They'd been traveling a little over thirty miles an hour, but not much more than that. Nearly four miles. Wherever the entrance was, it was a ways from where they needed to be.

That meant all the cars were illegally obtained to keep their existence an absolute secret. Someone who lived here enjoyed the dark side of keeping their actions under the radar.

Or they just really liked tunnels.

The car slowed to a stop beside an arched doorway carved out of the stone walls. Double dark wood doors with iron ornamentation opened.

A man in a suit with an earpiece stood in the doorway.

Thirty-three miles per hour for seven minutes meant they'd gone...three point eight five miles. If they'd only been going thirty-two miles per hour for the same seven minutes, that wouldn't shave much off the distance they'd traveled. If he had constructed something like this, he'd have used round numbers.

To get two miles of travel, that would be five minutes at twenty-four miles per hour. Who wanted to go that slow, really?

One of the men tugged on his arm.

His mind filled with the image of Cat's arm, covered in blood. She wasn't dead. She couldn't be. Even if he was killed in some horrifically gruesome way, she would live.

That was the important thing. She had to live because it didn't matter what happened to him. If he died, it would only be justice for the things he'd done.

You will keep her safe, won't You? You'll do that even if I'm dead?

Unlike last time, he was willing to focus on the fact God was real. God could hear him, and He would act on Simon's behalf. None of that was in question this time. If he was honest with himself, he'd known it all along. *You are therefore without excuse...*

He'd been running for far too long.

Running from God.

Running from the truth of who he was.

At seventeen, he'd been unable to think of anything but the blind terror. The threat of death, or worse. Given everything that'd happened in the past six or so years, it didn't surprise him to find that he wasn't the same scared kid. The boy he'd been the first time he was taken still lived inside him, but he was also a grown adult at the same time. It was an odd dichotomy of who he wanted to be and the truth of who he could turn into at any moment if he lost faith in himself or his family and friends or God.

It was all there, inside his mind.

If he focused hard enough, he could hear Peter's voice talking in a low, comforting tone, praying for their meal. He could hear his mother in the kitchen, making soup and singing a hymn.

The men had walked him up several flights of stairs, enough that his thighs were beginning to burn. The floor under his tennis shoes had turned from concrete to a thick rug that probably cost more than his car.

A chandelier hung from the ceiling.

Paintings decorated one wall, people from years past all looking super uptight in their Sunday best. Someone had their hand on someone else's shoulder in every family portrait. Each one had a thick gold filigree frame.

Across the room, a stout glass clinked against a whiskey decanter. The tall man pouring his own drink had on white linen pants and a powder-blue collared T-shirt with three buttons. His biceps were tanned like someone who played more golf than they worked. Rings on at least two fingers. A gold watch. Hair that had been styled with mousse and was mostly blonde but with some streaks of gray he probably left there on purpose.

"Simon Olson." He rounded the armchair over to the right, high-backed and burgundy-colored with wood edging.

"Lance North." He stared the guy down. How could anyone who saw him on social media or even at some event or in his office believe he wasn't evil to the core? It lived there in his eyes like a living, breathing thing. Waiting to strike.

Lance's expression remained impassive, as though Simon was an ant on the sidewalk in front of him. "So you do know who I am."

"You're the guy who terrorized Catalina Alvarez and made her bleed." He rolled his shoulders. They hadn't even tied him up this time. What did they want?

If God was on board with Simon's plan to shut down the whole network, that meant the server was housed here on this estate. Where North could keep an eye on it when he was here. But how could Simon find it in what was likely a maze of rooms—especially if these men were chasing him while he searched?

"Ah yes, your girlfriend. Nice woman. Didn't want to exchange herself to save one of the girls, though." He sipped from the amber liquid in his short glass.

If only Simon could steal it from him, slam the drink back in one go, and then start a fight. Instead, he kept himself still. Stayed where he was. Controlled himself. *Please, Lord.* God could pitch in anytime... Anytime... Now...

But that wasn't how it worked, was it? God didn't magically set the curtains on fire or cause the fire alarm to go off.

But if he could pull the alarm and then run for the server —wherever it was—maybe he had a shot at taking it down. Destroying the whole phone system by destroying the hardware that housed the program. If he could find the physical server he could do some serious damage.

Fire sounded pretty good right now—assuming he could find fuel and a way to start a blaze. If God wanted to make a way for Simon to do all that, he'd be totally on board with fixing everything.

First, Simon needed to get this conversation moving along so he could get to the plan where he stuck a wrench in North's entire empire. "What do you want?"

Lance North flashed a few perfect white teeth. "I do, in fact, have a job for you."

Big surprise. "What is it?"

"An upgrade, as it were." Lance settled onto one end of a ridiculous couch. Same burgundy velvet and wood accents. It looked uncomfortable.

Simon said nothing, letting him explain because the man liked the sound of his own voice so much.

"My company has secured exclusive use of a botnet." Lance sipped. "You're going to transfer hosting from my single centralized server to this botnet. The network will continue to function and be even more untraceable when you add a program that assures me of a rotating connection algorithm."

Of course he would.

Actually, it was pretty smart to move it from one server in a particular geographical location to distributed servers. Simon had been trying to find the site so he could destroy it and take down the whole network. That was a serious vulnerability.

If he moved the communication network to be hosted on a distributed server, that would spread it across the globe since the botnet would worm its way through the internet and find existing cloud infrastructure. The botnet would piggyback off other servers, and they would never know the network was there.

If law enforcement ever got wind of it, by the time they connected the dots—figuratively and literally—the network would have moved to a new series of servers, and they would never find it.

Even Simon wouldn't be able to find it.

"The fact you believe it's a good idea speaks volumes." Sip. "I'm assured it's the best option for continued success, and it all comes down to you."

Simon couldn't jump on the idea, not just because his expression was apparently giving away far too much.

It would be too obvious if he came across as eager to do the job—just so he could get access to the internet and the chance to wreck it all. But if he could get to the server, he could destroy the hardware before the transfer happened, and the network would be crispy burned toast.

Simon asked, "Why would I help you continue to commit crimes?"

Lance shifted on the seat. "Perhaps because last time you were here, you committed murder. What is the statute on that crime? Because I have all the evidence, and I can hand it over to that brother-in-law of yours. You'll go to prison for life."

"It was self-defense." Simon clenched his teeth. He refused to talk about that guy and what had nearly happened the day he escaped. A trauma group was one thing; this was something entirely different.

"When I'm done telling the story, you'll be a tortured young man raised by a monster and trained to kill for pleasure."

Simon pressed his lips together. In the court of public opinion, whose word would hold more weight? A do-gooder philanthropist or one young man with a rough past? Everything he'd been taught to believe about himself rushed back to the forefront.

But God...

At the same time, he could hear his mother's voice talking about being precious in His sight. Loved. Cherished.

Not something a preteen boy was necessarily interested in. At least, not then. Now it all washed back over him, making him wonder if this peace was a result of Peter or Cat— or both of them—praying for him.

"My men will escort you to the room where you'll be working. You will write a functional rotating connection algo-rithm, move the network from my server to the botnet, and successfully test the system. In three days."

Simon said, "There's no way I can get it done that fast."

Lance stood. He dug a hand into his pocket and pulled

out a small square of thin paper. He dropped it on the coffee table.

Dark ink, and lighter spots. An ultrasound? That's what the image looked like.

"Your sister."

Simon jerked his head up and pinned the guy with a stare.

"They haven't told anyone yet. It's still early, you know." Lance set his glass down on top of the ultrasound photo like it was a coaster. "Three days."

The men standing behind him grabbed Simon's arms and dragged him from the room.

TWENTY-NINE

Cat stood by her car at the hangar where they'd told her to wait. She watched the small airplane approach the runway, the only one that had landed in the last hour. Not much traffic at the municipal airport in the middle of the night.

Talia had told her they would charter a plane. That "the team" would be there as soon as they could get to Benson. All she'd had to do was tell Simon's friend that he was in trouble.

The name of the game seemed to be hurry up and wait, which was par for the course with most police work. Investigating a case to make sure nothing was missed and then waiting on a warrant. Cat wasn't so used to standing alone at an airport in the predawn hours.

The airplane landed, the flaps pushing against the air as it slowed. Tires braced against the asphalt, and the smell of burning rubber filled the air.

Cat pulled her jacket around her and flipped the collar up against the breeze. Even though it was in the midseventies out here right now, she was shivering.

The plane turned toward the hangar, taxiing toward her

car. She waited while they shut down, and then the door opened. Three men jogged down the steps, followed by an African American woman who picked her way down in heeled boots. All of them headed for her, so Cat pushed off the car and met them partway.

The first man was a former sergeant with the Benson PD. "Liam O'Connell?"

He grinned. "Catalina Alvarez." Liam pulled her into a hug.

He squeezed the wound on her arm, and she couldn't help the whimper. Couldn't bite it back fast enough.

He stepped back, an incredulous look on his face. "You're injured?"

"And Simon was kidnapped." She didn't mean to snap at him.

Liam didn't buy it. He had that older brother look Romeo got, which meant they would be talking about this later. "This is Niall and Josh."

Cat held out her left hand, and they made it work for a handshake.

Her right hand remained in her pocket.

"And this is Talia."

The woman they'd brought—or the woman who had brought them—came all the way up to her and touched Cat's cheeks. "Girl." She kissed Cat on the forehead. "Let's save your man."

Cat hadn't even told Talia what was going on between her and Simon. She must've figured it out somehow. Or Simon had mentioned Cat. "I brought the phone."

Liam said, "Hand it to Talia. Then show me your injury."

Talia's brows rose. Cat set the phone in her outstretched palm, but it was clear that wasn't Talia's biggest concern. "You're injured, girl? You should've said something."

Cat didn't want to explain what had happened in the van when Simon had been abducted, but there was no point in holding back information that might prove useful. So, she told them all of it, including how Peter and Jasper were working on it as Vanguard, and Romeo had told her to go home.

Liam said, "I'll check in with them."

But he didn't get out his phone or move at all.

Instead, he asked, "So you thought it was a good idea to go off on your own and save Simon?"

"I knew Talia would want to know that he had been taken." That sounded good, right? "And if you guys need backup, I can shoot as accurately with my left hand as I can with my right."

"Hmm." Liam didn't look all that convinced.

"You were right to call. I don't just want to know. I can help." Talia squeezed Cat's good hand. "We'll get him back, and if those Vanguard boys wanna help out on a federal operation, then we won't turn them down."

One of the other two men snorted.

"What do we do?" Cat bit her lip. "There's no way to find him with the network, right? It won't show us GPS."

"Let's go to the car, and we'll talk it through." Talia waved her to the hangar where the pilot walked around under the plane, looking at something or other. An SUV was parked in the corner.

The other two men, Niall and Josh, headed back onto the plane. They reappeared a few seconds later carrying plastic crates, which they set in the back of the SUV and popped open. Niall tossed Liam a bulletproof vest.

Liam lowered it over his head. "Take off your jacket."

Cat mashed her lips together but did it one-handed, sliding the jacket down off her right arm without wincing too much.

"Stitches?"

Because she'd been to a doctor? Cat said, "Jasper cleaned it and wrapped it with a bandage."

Liam didn't look happy. He waved his fingers at Josh, who tossed another vest over. He had her shift her arm so he could lower it over her head, and then he secured the tabs on her sides. "Talia, do you have anything that would work as a sling?"

Josh loaded a pistol and holstered it on his hip, then handed a rifle to Niall along with a clip.

"Try this." Talia came up with a scarf from her purse, purple with a silver pattern. She lifted Cat's arm with it, tucking her forearm against her front, and then tied the scarf behind her neck.

Liam got a pistol from Josh. "Left hand?"

Cat held it out.

"This will velcro to the front of the vest." He slid the gun into a holster and gave it to her.

Cat pressed it against the fuzzy material on the front of the vest. "Okay, we're ready to go. But we have no idea *where*."

Niall said, "That's why the plane didn't leave. We have no idea where they took him."

"To the estate where he was held the first time."

Talia shrugged. "Maybe. Maybe not."

"So what do we do?"

"We pray." Liam shrugged. As if it was as simple as that.

In a lot of ways, it was. But she also wanted to kick down some doors and find Simon. For some reason, her thinking that was amusing to them. Apparently, being injured and exhausted meant she had no filter on her face. "Talia?"

Talia handed the phone back, unlocked now. "I already put in the number. Send a message to it that he would know could only come from you. It'll be delivered to every number on the network at the same time. If Simon has access to the system—which I have to believe he does because why else would they grab him—then he'll see it. He can use it to tell us where he is."

Cat turned and paced away a couple of steps. They were already gearing up, maybe because it was all they could do. Be ready even if they didn't know where to aim. When it came to *fire*, they would be beyond prepared.

She didn't think it through too much. Something he'd know came from her...

The stars are bright tonight. Wish you could see them.

Maybe her mind was too tired to come up with something better. Or it was benign enough no one else would think anything of it other than that they'd received a message from a wrong number. How often did that happen on the network?

"Done." She held the phone back out, but Talia didn't make a move to take it.

The stylish woman—seriously, who was this put together in the middle of the night—opened her laptop on the hood of the SUV and began typing as fast as Simon usually did.

Cat stomped one foot on the ground, then the other, trying to inject some energy into her body. Her phone started to ring in her pocket, so she slid it out. Great. Romeo was calling. Probably to ask why she'd never showed up at their parents'. She sent him to voicemail. Once they had a location, they would call and tell Vanguard where to be. Until then, there was nothing to say to him.

"Got 'im." Talia kept typing. "He saw the message. He's on the network, but his permissions are limited. They've got him on lockdown. He sent me a code."

Cat glanced at the three men, who simply stood waiting. Evidently, this wasn't anything new for them, having to wait around for Talia to tell them which direction to shoot.

"We have coordinates." She lifted the laptop off the hood. "Let's go."

Talia climbed in the front seat.

Liam went around to the driver's side. Cat got in behind Talia but moved to the third row when the other two men got in behind her.

Cat asked, "Can you send them to me, and I'll pass them on to Peter and Romeo?"

Josh twisted in his seat, clicking in his seat belt. "Simon's brother and yours?"

She nodded. Her phone pinged.

"Sent."

Cat stared at it.

Josh said, "You should be used to that stuff with Simon in your life."

"It hasn't been long enough, maybe?"

"How long has it been?" Niall asked.

Cat buckled her own seat belt. "A few days."

She shook her head. How had it not been longer? Her arm hurt, she was exhausted, and the temptation to be grumpy was strong. She was craving pizza, if she was honest. Maybe one of these guys had a protein bar.

Talia said, "It's an hour's drive, so get some sleep."

Niall shifted lower in his seat, stretching out his knees. "Few days always seems like longer in the beginning."

Josh snorted. "Then a few years go by, and you can hardly remember a time before they were in your life."

Niall grinned at his friend.

Liam said, "Then a terrorist you thought was dead is threatening the country, and everyone you know is looking for nukes. You get blown up, she thinks you're dead, and you end up running all over Wyoming together trying to eliminate the threat."

Dead silence filled the cab of the SUV.

Josh started to chuckle. "Um…" He glanced at Cat with a wide smile on his face.

"I'm good, thanks." She grinned, texting her brother the information they'd found. It was better to arrange the wording in a text rather than have to listen to him demand to know why she wasn't safe. *Because life isn't safe.*

Safety was a misnomer as far as she could see.

And with a threat like Liam had described—a man who had terrorized Simon for years—there was no sitting back and letting other people take care of this.

Sometime later, after the sun had started to lighten the expanse of the sky to the east, Niall handed Cat a water bottle and a protein bar. She ate both while she woke up, listening to Liam and Talia discuss entrances.

The gun that was still stuck to the front of the vest she wore made her feel better, but sleeping in a vest wasn't something she planned to do again.

Josh handed her a couple of orange pills for the pain. She swallowed them down, then asked for two more. He handed them over. "Let's go."

"You wanna walk in the front door and immediately announce our presence?" Liam turned in his seat like a dad telling the kids to quiet down. "We need stealth."

We need to get Simon back.

Another car pulled up behind them. Up ahead stretched a long highway lined with tall pines on both sides, but on one side, they were completely black as if they'd been burned in a wildfire. The fire must not have jumped the road because the other side was green and healthy-looking.

Romeo and Peter got out of the car. Behind that car, two more men appeared.

More Vanguard operatives.

She spotted River Gaines and Samantha Jesse. Bob Davis, the older Vanguard agent. Jasper and Gage. Yet more people followed them that she didn't know.

Cat climbed out of the SUV. Romeo eyed the vest and gun and said, "So there's at least a chance you'll survive this."

Niall and Josh moved to stand on either side of her, as if to protect her from the rest of the people gathering around.

Liam said, "Okay, people. Let's go."

He went first into the trees.

Cat whispered a prayer, and they all followed him.

THIRTY

Simon's fingers paused over the keyboard. *Hope that wasn't North trying to trick me.* Fear wanted to overwhelm his hope, but it had been hours, and the chance of being rescued lessened with every passing tick of the clock on the wall.

That relentless *tick tick* drove him crazy. He was about to rip the clock off the wall and shatter it.

His brother had owned a clock like that once. It hung on the wall and kept Simon awake all night until he took the battery out. He suggested throwing the thing in the trash, but Peter just moved it to another room.

The guy would sleep through a tornado...or an earthquake.

He expected the door to fling open at any moment.

They'd shoved him into a tiny room that might as well be a storage closet or a prison cell. No window. Bare walls that hadn't even been painted. The seams where the drywall met had tape over them but nothing else. It looked like an unfinished basement room. A bulb hung from the ceiling. Even the light switch didn't have a cover on it, just the switch and the wires behind it and the square cut out of the drywall.

The metal desk was cold under his forearms. They'd taken his shoes—why? As if he was going to hang himself with his shoelaces. Or use a sneaker as a weapon? So bizarre.

His mind decided to settle on odd things like that, considering them for a while. Turning the idea over and over in his mind.

"Maybe you should focus on what you're doing instead of daydreaming." The man stood in front of the desk.

Simon shifted on the chair, just a stool and a thin back made of wood. It rolled two inches. It was irritating having to roll it back to the desk every time he shifted. "I'm figuring out a complex problem. It takes time and a whole lot of staring."

The guy didn't move. He just stared down at Simon with his shiny head and gray stubble on his cheeks. He had a scar above one eyebrow and dark blue eyes, almost gray.

"Are you going to stand there for three days until I'm finished?"

The guy said, "If that's what it takes."

Simon bit back a retort and wrote another line of code. Some of them were legit, others didn't make any sense. If Lance could see what he was doing, he might not think anything of it. Simon could be trying out ideas or working out things that obviously wouldn't work to get them off the table. His process was his process.

Problem was, he couldn't simply stall and wait for help to arrive. If he pushed it too far, held off on actually making progress on the task, then they'd kill him because he'd already failed.

There wasn't enough accessibility on the computer they'd given him to even get to the internet. All he could access were the server that hosted the communication network—where he'd seen the message that had to be from Cat—and the software to write the rotating connection algorithm.

Somewhere at the other end of the building, an explosion rocked the structure.

Dust drifted down from the ceiling.

The man standing on the other side of the desk turned to watch the tiny particles of the ceiling fall like the first flakes of snow.

Hope flared inside Simon like gasoline poured on a fire that came to life in a rush. Help was here.

The guard slid his gun from the holster under his left arm. He also had a stun gun on his belt and a knife. Simon had nothing but his jeans and the T-shirt he'd put on...however long ago that was.

Gunfire in the distance pricked his awareness, breaking through the thundering thoughts. The disbelief. The hope. The fear. All of it swirled in his mind, creating a rushing in his ears.

The guard pulled out a phone. He paced where he could see Simon as he waited.

No one answered.

He went to the door but paused and didn't open it.

When the guy turned back to Simon, he immediately started typing again. Working the problem and making it look like maybe he hadn't even recognized that something was happening. For all this guy knew, Simon thought an explosion and the sound of gunfire were normal for this place.

Maybe they were.

But the guard was getting concerned. Jiggling his knee as he stood there, then shifting his weight.

A door slammed down the hall.

Someone screamed, high-pitched, but it could be either male or female. A gun went off.

Simon kept typing, setting up a quick command he had preset into the communication network. A command that only proximity to the server would allow him to initiate. Being kidnapped and brought here meant he could do this.

If he could get to a terminal in the server room.

From this computer, he could start the process. It could only be completed at the source.

Simon finished typing it and went to press Enter.

The guard stomped over, dragged Simon out of the chair, and pressed the gun against his temple.

The door flung open, and Peter appeared. Out of breath. Sweat on his hairline, and pink cheeks. He'd fought his way down here to save Simon and, given the blood on his shirt, someone had been hurt.

Simon gasped in a breath. *Oh, no.* This wasn't good. His brother had a thunderous expression on his face.

Peter lifted his gun and pointed it over Simon's shoulder. "Let him go."

"I'd rather shoot him and then you," the man said.

Simon winced, not just because of what he'd said but also because of the harsh press of the gun against his temple. Peter couldn't fire. There was too much risk that he would miss even just a fraction and hit something other than the target. Putting a bullet in this guy might cause a reflexive squeeze of his finger on the trigger aimed at Simon's head.

His brother's gaze shifted. Just a fraction. Maybe not even visible to anyone else.

Simon blinked once slowly.

Two seconds later, he went limp, flopping down and narrowly missing hitting his chin on the desk. The gun glanced off his skull. The grip on his arm pulled his elbow up.

Before his butt hit the floor, Peter's gun went off.

The man who'd been holding him jerked, and his gun

went off, too. The round embedded itself in the computer monitor. Simon flinched. The guy dropped to the floor with a hole in his head.

"You okay?"

Simon didn't answer right away. He was busy trying to catch his breath, and he wasn't going to waste air on answering a dumb question. He was *not* okay.

He lifted his hand and managed to point at the computer.

"It's toast. The screen is smoking."

"Hit Enter. Pray you didn't mess the whole thing up."

Peter hissed out a quick puff of air. "As if that would be my fault." He jabbed the Enter button. "Up?"

Simon lifted his hand, and his brother grabbed his wrist. Simon did the same, and Peter hauled him to his feet.

"Is this when we hug it out?"

Simon said, "We need to shut down the system first."

"No time for hugs?"

Simon slapped him on the back. "I can't believe you choose to do this for a living."

Peter grinned. "It's great."

The guy looked like he was high on adrenaline. Simon said, "We need to get to the server room. I have no idea where it is."

Peter said, "Someone must've found it. We're raiding the whole place. Vanguard, a bunch of cops—but don't tell Russ they're out of their jurisdiction—and some Northwest Counter-Terrorism agents."

"Talia?"

"Yep. Liam, and two guys as well. Cat brought them."

Simon stopped. "She's here?"

Peter stuck his head out of the door and looked both ways. "Clear!"

Someone out in the hall yelled back, "Clear!"

"Someone get Cat down here!" Peter stepped into the hall. "And find out where the server room is."

Simon left the room where they'd held him and looked both directions. To the right was a wall at the end, no window or decorations. Rooms on both sides. To the left was a set of wooden stairs they'd used.

Peter's phone rang. "Olson." He glanced at Simon. "Got it." As soon as he hung up, Peter said, "The server room is on the other side of the house. And Cat's in trouble. She ran into North, and Romeo can't get to her."

"Let's go."

Peter nodded, and they ran for the stairs.

THIRTY-ONE

The world around Cat was nothing but black. Pitch black so dark she couldn't see her hand in front of her face.

All she could hear were the sounds of her own breaths and the distant echo of pounding footsteps.

She stretched out her good hand and took measured steps toward the wall she'd seen right before the door behind her had clicked shut. She would be able to find the door after she found the wall and traced it back to the corner. Right now, she needed something tangible to hold on to instead of all this blank nothingness. An absence of light.

Her fingers glanced off the wall, and she settled her palm on it, then leaned against it and tugged out her phone. No signal? Of course.

Of course.

The dull ache on the outside of her arm was enough to distract her and make her even more irritated by this whole thing. Why couldn't she just have found Simon already?

Why did it have to be this difficult?

Cat stowed the phone in her back pocket and moved toward the door. She found the edge, then felt for the handle.

It wouldn't budge.

She rattled the handle and pounded on the heavy door. How could she hear nothing from the other side? It had to be reinforced in some way, more than a normal fire door. What was this place?

She'd been working her way through the house with Romeo behind her, gun out. He'd followed every turn she'd made, and Cat had said nothing. If he wanted to be the one to watch her back, she wasn't going to complain. Just as long as they retrieved Simon and stopped Lance North.

Romeo had been there, not two steps back.

She'd seen Lance at the end of the hall and ran as fast as she could toward him, her arm tucked against her side with the sling. Romeo had called out to her right as she eased up on the door and slid in with measured steps the way she'd been trained to. She'd run in here after Lance, and then the door had shut.

Her on one side, Romeo on the other.

Where had Lance gone?

She pulled as hard as she could on the handle, and nothing happened. If she couldn't go that way, did she need to follow the direction Lance went to get out of here? She had no choice except to venture into the pitch black. It was that or sit around and wait for rescue.

Not when a bad guy was getting away.

Cat found the wall so she could lean her good arm on it. Not great since it restricted her movement. But better than crashing into a wall and being in so much pain she passed out.

She started toward the far end of the hallway. Tunnel. What was this place?

Cat hadn't walked far before she spotted twin lights heading toward her. Headlights? She didn't hear a car engine.

The vehicle sped toward her, and the brakes whined.

How many shots had she expended so far tonight? She had fired at least three. Why hadn't she counted them?

She held the gun up while the car slowed in front of her.

The driver's door opened, and Lance rushed out. She followed him with her gun hand, squeezing the trigger. Each flash from her muzzle lit the tunnel like a beacon. She turned the gun and pulled the trigger at point-blank range.

The gun clicked. No flash.

Lance raced toward her.

He slammed into her and Cat hit the ground. All the air expelled from her lungs. Why hadn't he simply escaped? He'd come back for her? It made no sense.

But asking herself inane questions she had no answers to was better than thinking about the pain screaming through her.

No, that was her screaming.

He cuffed her across the face. "Shut up. Get in the car. You'll have to do."

Lance grabbed her arms, gripping the wound on her right arm. Cat screamed again. "I said, shut up."

She swallowed, choking on her own sob.

He shoved her at the car, opened the door, and pushed her in. She twisted around and kicked at the door with both feet. He leaned on it and shoved her knees to her chest. The door clicked.

As soon as he rounded the front end, she grabbed the handle and yanked it.

The door swung open and hit the concrete wall.

Cat jumped out of the car and ran.

She tore down the tunnel, her hand sliding along the wall.

Run. His footfalls pounded on the floor behind her. Echoing toward her. The relentless, punishing pace was enough to make her go insane.

Whatever he'd come back for...he wasn't getting it from her.

Clean living, exercise, and the strength that came from Christ were going to win out. She had to believe that despite her injuries, she could be faster than him. Cat settled into a rhythm in the same way she did when she ran with Romeo, finding her stride and the zone where she could even increase her speed.

The frantic pace of terror settled into a sprint she could sustain for a while.

Lance let out a frustrated sound behind her.

Cat smiled to herself. *I guess I'll have to thank Romeo for making me run faster than I want.* And she would have something to be thankful to God for. Plenty.

Light in the distance grew closer. She forced her mind to keep laser-sharp attention on it, not on the dark all around her. How long had she been running?

Was this a way out?

Lord, go with me.

She knew He did and always would, but asking made her feel better.

First thing that changed was an awareness of a noise. Over the rush of each breath in her ears, Cat heard a rhythmic beeping.

The tunnel opened into a garage.

She stumbled while trying to slow down. Sweat laced her hairline and dripped down her back. Noise behind her in the tunnel meant he was still coming. She looked around for a weapon but saw no tools. Could she steal a car? She didn't know how to hotwire anything, and was that even possible for a high-end sports car? She'd never worked those cases.

Lance ran out of the tunnel and stopped fifteen feet from her. "It doesn't matter. You'll be my prize."

Cat shook her head.

"There isn't much time. We'll go. You can pay me what I'm owed later." He sneered at her; his eyes gleaming with something horrible. "And for a long time to come."

Cat backed up. "I'm not going anywhere with you."

"You expect me to leave with nothing to show for it?" He huffed a laugh, but it contained no humor. "I don't think so. The Olsons cost me everything I had here. So, you're going to repay that debt."

Simon. Peter.

Cat took a few more steps back.

"Or we can start right now." Lance took a step closer. "While the house is destroyed, you'll give me a pound of flesh. Because it's me or you burn with them."

She sucked in a choppy breath. "You set the house on fire?"

He took another step toward her. "Fail-safe charges. In case the empire falls."

Everyone in the house...

All those people...

"Stop it. Turn it off." He was going to kill them all.

Lance chuckled. He rushed her, and her back hit a car. He slammed her up against it and put both hands around her neck.

His thick fingers squeezed the breath from her throat.

Cat choked against it, trying to breathe but unable to get air. Her injured arm was trapped between them. She slapped with her free one at his shoulder, his head, his hands. It was as if he didn't even notice.

Spots erupted at the edges of her awareness.

Her body lost the ability to hold her up.

He kept squeezing, and all she could see was the evil look in his eyes.

What was he going to do to her? She didn't want to know. *Lord...* Her thoughts shuttered, and her mind blanked.

She heard someone roar, and Lance was dragged away from her.

Cat fell to her hands and knees on the ground, gasping and coughing. Someone steadied her, holding her gently and taking care with her injuries.

A man said, "Lie down for me. Easy now."

Her forehead touched the cold concrete floor.

A few feet away, Lance lay on his back. Simon was on him, punching Lance in the face over and over again.

The man by her said, "That's enough."

Peter stood beyond Simon, a deadly look on his face. "He's almost done. He's just working something out."

Jasper was the one with her. She managed to focus on his face long enough to figure that out. Simon's boss said, "Enough!"

Cat flinched.

"She needs an ambulance."

Simon got up, easing to his feet, blood on his fists. He pushed back his hair, leaving blood in the strands. "We'll take one of these cars."

"Charges." The word was barely audible. Did they hear her?

Peter went for a rack of key fobs on the wall. "Lamborghini or Porche?"

Cat whispered, "Charges."

Jasper leaned down. "What was that?"

"Watch out." Simon patted his boss's shoulder.

Jasper said, "She's trying to say something."

Both of them leaned close. Cat said, "House...explode."

Simon flinched.

Jasper rocked back and stood. "Get everyone out of the house. It's rigged to blow."

Someone lifted her into their arms, and everything went black.

EPILOGUE

Three months later.

Simon tugged on the end of the bow tie. This side room in the small country church in a little town on the coast echoed with instrumental worship music being piped into all the rooms.

"Leave it. It looks good." Talia swatted his hand.

He frowned. "It looks ridiculous. I just can't decide if I look like a monkey or a penguin. Why is it called a monkey suit anyway?"

Talia rolled her eyes, and her gold eyeshadow glinted in the light. The door opened. Mason, her husband, stuck his head in—the guy was as big as a Redwood and had a kid on each hip. He wore a suit, though probably one of the same ones he wore every day since he worked as a Secret Service agent. Their four-year-old son was in a suit of his own, and the little girl had on a pink dress.

A different door opened, and Peter stepped out of the washroom, tucking in the tail of his shirt. He'd gelled his hair and complained only a little when Simon refused to get more than a trim. "Ready."

Simon nodded. Why was he nervous anyway? He wasn't the one getting married.

Mason said, "Let's go, babe. The natives are getting restless."

Talia kissed Simon on the cheek. "You'll be fine."

Peter shrugged on his suit jacket and held his hands out, palms up. "What about me? I'm the one getting married."

"Boy, you already know you'll be fine."

Peter had to concede that point.

Simon took in the scene. Talia gave his brother a kiss on the cheek and said, "Your mother would be very proud of you."

Then she trailed to the door and closed it.

Peter looked at him. *She's right.* Neither of them said anything, sharing the moment in the quiet with their own thoughts even if the sentiment was the same for both of them.

There was a gentle knock on the door.

"Come in." Peter walked over to it, glancing at his watch.

Their sister Freya stepped in. She wore a blue dress cut to accommodate the fact she was now in the second trimester of pregnancy. Though, it wasn't super noticeable. Mostly, she just seemed to have this...glow about her. Her dark eyes shone like the pins she had holding back her hair. Her eyes filled with tears. "Wow."

Simon and Peter both strode to her, hugging her between them.

"I'm not supposed to cry."

Simon snorted.

Peter said, "Who cares? Cry if you wanna cry."

"Where is Lucas, anyway?" Simon half expected him to be here. The guy practically rolled out the red carpet everywhere she went now that she was carrying their baby. She could barely lift her purse without him offering to help.

Peter made the same noise Simon had a second ago.

Freya smacked his shoulder, but it was weak. "Well, it's almost time. Your ladies are waiting for you. I should take my seat."

Peter said, "Love you," and kissed her cheek.

"Same." Simon leaned down.

She smacked his shoulder.

"Fine. Love you." He kissed her cheek as well.

Freya sniffed. "I love you both, too. I'm proud to be your sister and that you'll be this baby's uncles. But don't be surprised that I thanked God on my knees it wasn't twins." She squeezed both their arms and headed out.

Peter followed her, and Simon shut the door behind him.

Catalina stood in the hallway. Peter said something to her that was too quiet for him to hear and kissed her cheek. Then he continued on, using the side door to enter the little sanctuary.

She lifted her gaze to him, eyeing him appreciatively. "It turned out nice. You look good."

He frowned, rolling his shoulders. "I feel ridiculous."

She giggled.

"You're the one that looks good."

She'd been self-conscious about the graze on her arm being a visible scar that would mar the occasion, but so many of them had scars that they'd convinced her it just made her one of them to have survived something that could've killed her.

Fortunately, she hadn't settled on the square-necked dress with sleeves to her elbows.

"We should go."

He tore his gaze away from her collarbones. "Hmm?"

Cat chuckled. "Come on. Or we'll miss it."

She wrapped her arm in his, and they headed for the lobby. Simon got a look at Selena across the other side of the entrance, where the hallway to her dressing room had been. He touched a hand to his chest and stopped. His eyebrows rose as he took in her gown. The whole package. "Wow."

She smiled wide.

Cat said, "Seriously. I hope I look half that good when we..." Her voice trailed off. "Uh..."

Simon tugged her to face him. "Is this where I tell you that you'd look good in a garbage sack?"

"That's true. I would."

"Or one of those itchy potato sacks. Or a cardboard box with arm holes."

"It would have to be a pretty big box."

"When we..." He smiled. "You know."

She lifted up on her toes and kissed him. "I know."

"Good."

As far as he was concerned, that pretty much settled it. They would get married sooner or later. She would look amazing. He would try not to be uncomfortable in whatever he wore. The preacher would unite them in front of God and the people who RSVP'd.

Life would go on.

They'd have families of their own.

Births. Deaths. Happiness. Hopefully, not too much tragedy. Through it all, God would still be good. And good *to* them.

Selena clapped, and her entourage snapped into gear. "Let's go people. Let's get this show on the road."

Simon chuckled. Cat slid her arm through his, and they

stepped into the sanctuary, walking down the aisle to a sweet hymn of thankfulness. He kissed her, and she took her seat, then he went to stand with his brother.

Peter pulled him into a bone-crushing hug.

And then the wedding march began.

KEEP READING FOR...

- Where to find more great Lisa Phillips books.

- How to sign up for Lisa's newsletter and get a FREE book.

- Where to find Lisa on social media.

ABOUT THE AUTHOR

Find out more about Lisa Phillips at her website, where you'll discover more romantic suspense fan-favorite series and heart-pounding thriller novels.
https://authorlisaphillips.com/about/

If you loved this book, please consider sharing about it on social media. Or leave a review at your book retailer website, on Goodreads, or on Bookbub. Your review will help others find great books to entertain and encourage them!

For a FREE novel from Lisa Phillips, scan the QR code below to connect to Lisa's newsletter and be the first to hear about sales, new books, and recommendations for your TBR pile.

Find Lisa on Social Media!

facebook.com/authorlisaphillips

instagram.com/lisaphillipsbks

bookbub.com/authors/lisa-phillips

ALSO BY LISA PHILLIPS

Find out more about Benson First Responders on the series page:

https://authorlisaphillips.com/product-tag/benson-first-responders/

Benson First Responders is a continuation of Last Chance Downrange. Read the whole Last Chance Downrange series now!

Point of Impact

Hard Target

Hollow Point

Terminal Velocity

Audio Available from Podium Publishing

Find more stories based in Last Chance County at:

https://authorlisaphillips.com/product-tag/last-chance-county/

Other series by Lisa:

Brand of Justice (Thriller series)

Benson First Responders (Christian Romantic Suspense)

Last Chance Fire & Rescue (Sunrise Publishing)

Chevalier Protection Specialists

Last Chance County

Northwest Counter-Terrorism Taskforce

Double Down

WITSEC Town (Sanctuary)

And numerous other titles including several from

Love Inspired Suspense.

Find the complete list here:

https://authorlisaphillips.com/all-books/